喚醒你的英文語感！

Get a Feel for English !

喚醒你的英文語感！

Get a Feel for English !

愈忙愈要學
英文簡報

作者／Quentin Brand

修練用簡報作秀的好習慣

看到 Quentin 老師這本《愈忙愈要學英文簡報》直覺聯想到第 864 期商業週刊封面的斗大標題：作秀是個好習慣。文中指出調查發現人們對你的印象，93% 來自外型、肢體語言和語調。而亞裔占美國人口的 4%，但《財星》500 大公司中，亞裔卻只占了 1%，只因為他們不懂「秀」。簡報也是一種作秀，尤其是英文簡報。Quentin 老師在本書一開頭也點明「無趣是成功簡報的頭號大敵」，簡報之所以無趣，英文表達的順暢度就是一大關鍵因素，做過英文簡報的人對這一點應該都有深刻的體會。

在本人教習英文簡報技巧八年的經驗中，確實目睹某些高階經理人用中文簡報時侃侃而談，但碰到英文簡報時卻瞠目結舌。這種像是由高材生變成低能兒的挫折感就出在英文簡報的高難度與複雜性。用英文做簡報不只牽涉到中翻英，更需要語氣、語調的配合以及流暢的英語表達。我非常認同 Quentin 老師所說「細節是非常重要的」，很多人事實上也因為對所說的英文正確度沒有信心，導致簡報效果大打折扣。仔細研讀 Quentin 老師收集的 set-phrases 絕對可以大幅降低細節的錯誤率，進而強化簡報時的自信度。

好好一個簡報就毀在英文上，那種槌心肝的致命感受或許可以因為 Quentin 老師這本書的問世而大幅改善。一般人可能認為用英文做簡報是高階經理人的事情、或要英文很好才能做英文簡報。實際狀況是很多外國人用英文做簡報也做得不怎樣。簡報絕對是需要專業訓練的。在外國，簡報訓練原本就是政府官員、CEO、高階經理人上台前的必修課程。反過來說用英文做簡報真是有竅門的。其中一大竅門就是熟讀常用的英文簡報用語，降低英文本身所造成的臨場障礙。能夠「出口成章」，肢體語言和眼神自然會流露出自在和自信心，做英文簡報自然有令人激賞的效果。

　　Quentin 老師將他十餘年來教簡報的經驗錦囊相授，有心的讀者隨便翻一翻這本書，就可知道這本書是來自於一個豐富教學經驗的老師，我本人也上過 Quentin 老師的英文簡報訓練，不得不對他的專業和敬業由衷佩服。在台灣有很多外國人奉獻自己，提供醫療服務照顧偏遠地區孤苦無依的人，在台北， Quentin 老師也用他的專業、熱誠幫助廣大的上班族，用最有效的方式學習、運用商業英文。 Quentin 老師在前一本書《愈忙愈要學英文 Email》引起很大的迴響後，再接再勵出版的《愈忙愈要學英文簡報》，真是台灣上班族的一大福音。

AIG 友邦國際信用卡股份有限公司
市場行銷部副總經理
卓文芬

推薦序

簡報技巧和簡報用語雙面兼顧

過去十多年來，我曾經為不同企業安排了上百場次的英語簡報課程，但大多著重在簡報技巧上的學習，而較少著墨在簡報的常用語。坊間並沒有人像 Quentin 一樣，兼顧了簡報技巧和簡報用語。

但自從 Quentin 的 Leximodel 字串學習法推廣以來，確實幫助了許多想學習英語的企業人士。他們可以運用簡單、架構性的簡報用語來做簡報，減少了事前準備的時間，並且能夠更有自信且專業地以英語展現自己和所代表的公司。

Quentin 過去僅有教授英文簡報的訓練課程，現在他把研究付梓出書，嘉惠了許多未能參加訓練課程的職場人士，實在是英語學習者的一大福音。

我誠摯地推薦這本書，它會是你在做英語簡報時一個很棒的指南！

澳威爾管理顧問公司
課程總監
陳亦芬

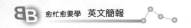

推薦序

英文表達更上層樓

等待了五年，Quentin 老師的英文教材終於付梓出版。除了要恭喜 Quentin 多年心血有成之外，我想真正有福的是廣大的讀者們，不須要再像過去的我，要花費千金才可追隨老師學習。現在，只須由本書淺顯詳盡的解說，即可一窺老師英語學習之秘，實乃可喜可賀也！

我自大學畢業起即在外商任職，加上留學的期間，英文早已成為主要的「謀生」工具。然而一直到接受 Quentin 的指導、開始接觸 Leximodel 之後，才在英語表達上有了突破。這才瞭解原來文法並不是英文的主體，傳統的英文學習方式，在不知不覺中已相當程度地侷限了學習者的思考模式，更加深了非母語學習者在學習上的文化障礙 (culture barrier)。Leximodel 的英語學習法突破了傳統的學習方式，並對「語言學習 vs. 文化差異」的議題提供了良好的思維方向。對我本身而言，有幸比讀者早幾年接觸 Leximodel，我的收穫實無法在此列舉。但我相信，讀者讀完此書，當與我有同感才是！

Quentin 老師是多才多藝的，彈得一手好鋼琴，對語言學、人類學亦有研究。雖然他上課堅持不說國語，但我知道他的國文造詣亦不差。我衷心期望他的知識可以透過著作，嘉惠更多的大眾！

美商甲骨文公司
大中華區產品全球化經理
劉靜蘋
（推薦序依姓氏筆畫排序）

輪到你上場了—— Are You Ready?

做商業簡報本來就不是一件容易的事，除了要充分了解業務的內容及簡報的對象，資料準備要詳盡，架構要清晰明朗，時間要能掌握之外，還要熟悉硬體操作，注意儀態與目光接觸等，沒有經驗的人不經過反覆練習，實在很難做得好。

如果要用英文做簡報，那可以說是難上加難了。未來台灣經濟會繼續走自由化、全球化的路線，以吸引外資來活化市場。這麼一來，職場上的英文能力就顯得更為重要了，而用英文做商業簡報、談判、或產品說明的機會也就愈來愈多了。

不過，光有英文口說能力，不一定能做好英文簡報。做簡報需要規劃、整合資訊、連貫內容各部份，配合聲光來表達，更不能忽略包裝語言。之前有一位電腦公司的年輕主管來找我幫忙修改他們公司的英文說明，曾經很感慨地說無論產品多優秀，英文說明不上軌道的話，對公司的專業形象及產品的可靠度都構成傷害，也間接影響國外買單。做英文簡報也一樣，除了內容要專業外，基本的文字包裝不能做不好。《愈忙愈要學英文簡報》一書就針對這方面的需求給讀者提供了一個具體而鍥而不捨的反覆練習相關簡報語言的機會。

這本書繼承了 Quentin 先生上一本暢銷書《愈忙愈要學英文 E-mail》的精神，用最明白清楚的章節安排及解說來帶領讀者按部就班地完成必要的英文簡報的準備工作。 Quentin 先生運用他獨創的 Leximodel 概念並配合大量的練習題目來幫讀者有效地掌握實用的簡報英文。開場白該如何說，遇到難纏的觀眾時又該如何回答問題？這些不同的習慣用語都被整齊地歸類到每一章節中供讀者學習參考。書中也適時提醒讀者要注意其他的簡報事項，諸如克服臨場焦慮、使用適量的圖表等等。

　　要能從這本書中獲取最大的幫助，先決條件是必須已經具備充實而正確的簡報內容。《愈忙愈要學英文簡報》教你簡報英文，但不教你簡報的內容，因為各人的工作性質不一，所以簡報的材料內容一定要自理。但是無論你賣的是哪一種產品，要發表的是多麼重要的策略或商業計畫，這本書都能增加你用英文做簡報的信心及語言專業度，使你的表現錦上添花。

　　特別提醒諸位，本書的第一部分的第二章中有連音的練習。連音固然能使你的英文聽來更悅耳或更道地，但應注意能連則連，沒有把握或功力還不到的人不能勉強，也不必為此感到氣餒或抱歉。勉強連音會使人口齒不清，咬字不正，嚴重影響溝通，甚至製造負面印象。英文口語表達清楚為第一要務，內容要正確，連音和句子的抑揚頓挫都可以慢慢學。

　　我在台灣大學的財金所教商用英文多年，從畢業同學的就業經驗深切體會到職場的專業容易學會，證照難不倒聰明人，但英文卻很難專精。若是專業和英文都一流、英文簡報嘎嘎叫的話，總經理的位置恐怕有一天非您莫屬。

Are you ready?

台灣大學外文系副教授

梁欣榮

C O N T E N T S

Unit 9 問答

結語 ◆◆◆◆◇

附錄 ◆◆◆◆◇

The Leximodel

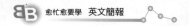

引言與學習目標

做簡報對所有的商場專業人士來說都是個考驗。無論你是新手，或是有經驗的商場人士，簡報都是你專業生涯裡的一部分。但是我們對做簡報都覺得很不自在。

用自己的母語做簡報已經不容易，以外國語言來進行更是難上加難。簡報的重點在於溝通，而用非母語來溝通要面對完全不同的問題。你需要學會完全不同的技巧和程序才能克服這些問題。況且你有個全新的焦點：**語言本身**。當你用自己的母語做簡報時，焦點在於想法以及組織、傳遞這些想法的方法上。你不會專注在語言上。不過，用非母語的語言來做簡報意味著你必須將語言作為準備的焦點。本書的重點在於簡報的用語。請看以下這個圖示：

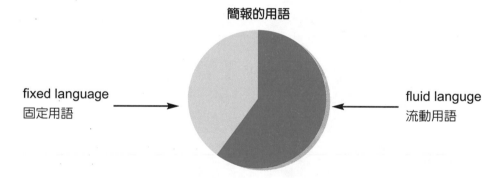

簡報的用語

fixed language
固定用語

fluid languge
流動用語

不管是哪一種簡報，有些用語是重複的，那就是你用來說明結構、組織想法以及段落轉折的用語，這些用語是固定的。然而，在你簡報裡說明資訊的用語（表達理念和內容的字彙）則是隨著簡報而有所不同，這些用語是會變動的。

本書的設計旨在協助各位熟練簡報的固定用語，並提供各位一些準備、練習、進行英文簡報的技巧。目的在讓各位的英文簡報能如中文簡報一樣專業。此外，本書也旨在協助各位提昇一般的英文能力。

現在請各位花一分鐘看看下列的問題，並寫下你的答案。

Task 1

想想下列的問題，並記下自己的答案。

1. 你為什麼買這本書？

2. 你想從中學到什麼？

3. 你在做英文簡報時碰到什麼困難？

　　請看下列這些可能的回答，並勾選和你想法最接近的答案。

1. 你為什麼購買本書？

　□ 我買這本書是為了學英文，用於專業。

　□ 我是個大忙人，不想浪費時間學工作上用不到的東西，更不想做些辦公室裡派
　　不上用場的語言練習。

　□ 我在這本書的封面上看到「英文簡報」一詞，我覺得自己的中文簡報很不錯，
　　不過常在想有沒有更好的方法可以進行英文簡報。

　□ 我想要一本有練習引導的書，而且還包含相關的參考要點。一本我能隨身攜
　　帶、參考的書，完全針對簡報所寫的手冊。

　□ 我想要一本了解我需求的書！

2. 你想從中學到什麼？

　□ 我想要學到工作上所需最常用的字彙和文法。

　□ 我想要學到組織簡報結構的正確方法。

　□ 我希望這本書像英文家教一樣，幫我指出錯誤，予以糾正。

　□ 我想要學國際性的英文，我有些客戶是英國人、有些是美國人，還有歐洲、印
　　度和東南亞的客戶。我希望所有的客戶都能理解我的簡報。

　□ 我覺得自己的英文簡報一定很無趣，我說得太慢，而且有時候對自己的發音沒
　　有信心。

　□ 我英文念得不好，也很討厭文法。對我而言，文法很無聊，而且比起對著滿屋
　　子的外國人做簡報還要令人害怕！可是偏偏文法很重要，我希望找到能改善我
　　的英文、而無須苦讀文法的方法。

　□ 我想找到自學英文的方法。我在英文的環境中工作，但自知沒有善加利用這個
　　優勢，加強專業英文能力。我希望這本書能讓我知道該怎麼做。

3. 你在做英文簡報時碰到什麼困難？

☐ 我不知道怎麼組織簡報的結構。我不知道如何向觀眾說明這些結構。

☐ 我覺得自己的英文簡報一定很無趣，因為觀眾通常會睡著。

☐ 我很討厭問答的部分，因為我不知道他們會提出哪些問題，而且有時候我不了解他們的問題。這種感覺真糟糕！

☐ 我希望自己的英文和中文一樣專業，可是我知道我的英文會讓自己失望，我的英文思考速度不夠快。

☐ 用英文做簡報給我很大的壓力，我常緊張到發抖的地步，我得加強對自己表現能力的信心。

☐ 我從來不知道自己的簡報成功與否。

☐ 準備簡報需要花好幾個小時，因為我不知道要如何開始、要放入哪些東西、該刪掉哪些資料。有沒有什麼指南可以幫助我？

☐ 我覺得我的英文還可以，可是我的簡報技巧糟糕透了。我不知道雙手要擺在哪裡、眼睛又該看哪裡，我在滿屋子的人前會覺得害羞，特別是當中有我的老闆時！

　　你可能認同以上敘述的部分、甚至是全部，你也可能有些我沒有想到的觀點。不過在此先讓我做個自我介紹。我是 Quentin Brand，我教導來自世界各地、像各位這樣的商場專業人士已經有十五年的歷史，其中大部分的時間是在台灣。我的客戶來自企業的各個階層，從大型跨國企業的分公司經理，到擁有海外市場的小型本地公司的新進實習人員，我的學生跨足商界各階層。每個人均曾吐露過上述的心聲。他們（包括你）共同的心願，就是找到簡單又實際的方法學英文。

　　各位，你們已經找到了！多年來，我為像各位這樣忙碌的商場人士研發出一套教導和學習英文的方法。這方法的核心概念叫做 Leximodel，是以全新的觀點來看待語言。現在 Leximodel 已被一些全世界最大、最成功的企業採用，藉此協助執行主管發揮他們最大的英文潛力。本書就是根據 Leximodel 為基礎。

　　「前言」的目的是介紹和教你運用 Leximodel。我也會解釋本書用法，以及如何從本書獲得最佳學習效果。看完本章，你應該達到的學習目標如下：

☐ 清楚了解何為 Leximodel、以及用 Leximodel 學英文的好處。

☐ 了解 chunks、set-phrases 和 word partnerships 的差別。

☐ 閱讀書信文章時，能夠辨認文中的 chunks、set-phrases 和 word partnerships。

☐ 知道學習 set-phrases 時會遇到哪些困難，以及如何克服這些困難。

☐ 清楚了解本書中的不同要素，以及如何運用這些要素。

在繼續往下看之前，我要先強調本書中 Task 對學習的重要性。各位在前面的部分應該已注意到，我會請各位停下來先做個 Task，回答一些問題。做完後，才繼續看下去，我希望各位在接下來的章節中也能照做。

每個章節各有許多 Task，這些 Task 都是經過縝密的設計，協助各位在不知不覺中吸收新的語言。做 Task 的思維過程要比答案的正確重要得多。所以各位務必要確實去做 Task，在完成之前不要先看答案。當然，為了節省時間，你大可不做 Task，一股作氣讀完整本書，但如此不啻是浪費時間罷了，因為你沒有進行充分發揮本書效果所需的思維訓練。請相信我的話，按部就班做 Task 準沒錯！

The Leximodel

可預測度

本節中我將介紹 Leximodel 字串學習法。字串學習法是用嶄新的觀點來看語言，這是基於非常簡單的理念：

Language consists of words which appear with other words.

語言是由字串構成的。

這概念簡單易懂，不過這當中的涵義是，與其把語言想成文法和字彙，我們可以把語言想成字串，也就是字的組合。為了讓各位明白我的意思，讓我們先做一個 Task，做完之後再繼續看下去。

Task 2

想一想，下列單字後面通常會搭配什麼字，請寫在空格中。

listen _____

depend　　　———————————

English　　　———————————

financial　　———————————

　　你可能在第一個單字旁邊填上 **to**，第二個單字旁邊填的是 **on**。我猜得沒錯吧？這是因為一套叫做「語料庫語言學」（corpus linguistics）的軟體程式和運算技巧，透過統計方式證實 listen 後面接著 to 的機率非常高（大約 98.9%）， depend 後面跟著 on 的機率也相差不遠。這表示 listen 和 depend 後面接的字幾乎千篇一律（listen 後面加 to， depend 後面加 on）。由於機率非常高，這兩個字串可以視為 fixed（固定字串）。因為它們是固定的，如果寫 listen 和 depend 兩個字時，後面沒有接 to 和 on，就很可能犯了錯誤。

　　接下來的兩個字 **English** 和 **financial** 後面該接什麼字比較難預測，所以我猜不出來你在這些字的旁邊寫了些什麼。然而，我可以在特定的範圍內猜，你可能在 English 旁邊寫的是 class、book、teacher、email、grammar 等，在 financial 旁寫的是 department、news、planning、product、problems 或 stability 等。卻無法像方才對前兩個字那麼篤定了。為什麼？這是因為要正確猜出 English 和 financial 旁邊的字，在統計上的機率要低得多，而且許多字的機率都相當。因此我們可以說 English 和 financial 的字串並不固定，稱之為 fluid（流動字串）。所以與其把語言想成文法和字彙，各位大可將語言視作一個龐大的語料庫，裡面的字串有的是固定的，有的則是流動的。根據可預測度，我們可以看出字串的固定性和流動性，見圖示：

The Spectrum of Predictability 可預測度

字串的可預測度是 Leximodel 的基礎，因此 Leximodel 的定義可以再加上一句：

Language consists of words which appear with other words. These combinations of words can be placed along a spectrum of predictability, with fixed combinations at one end, and fluid combinations at the other.

　　語言是由字串構成的。這些組合字串可以依其可預測的固定程度區隔，一邊是固定的組合，另外一邊則是流動性的組合。

Chunks、set-phrases 和 word partnerships

　　你可能會納悶：這對我有什麼幫助？我怎麼知道哪些字串是固定的、哪些是流動的，而且它們如何讓我更輕鬆地學英文？別急，放輕鬆，現在起英文會愈學愈上手。

　　字串（英文叫作 multi-word items，以下簡稱 MWI）可分成三大類：chunks、set-phrases 和 word partnerships。這些名詞沒有對等的中譯，所以請各位把這幾個英文字記起來。現在開始深入探討這三大類字串。你很快就會發現各類字串都易懂而好用。我們先看 MWI 的第一大類：chunks。Chunks 的字串有固定也有流動元素。listen to 即是個很好的例子：listen 後面總是跟著 to，這是固定元素；但有時 listen 可以是 are listening、listened、have not been listening carefully enough，這些則是 listen 的流動元素。give sth. to sb. 是另一個很好的例子：give 後面得接某物（sth.），然後 to 再加上某人（sb.）。因此 give sth. to sb. 在這裏是固定的字串。不過 give sth. to sb. 這個 chunk 中，sth. 和 sb. 這兩個位置可以使用的詞範圍可就廣了，例如 give a raise to your staff（給員工加薪）、give a presentation to your boss（向老闆做簡報）。請看以下圖示。

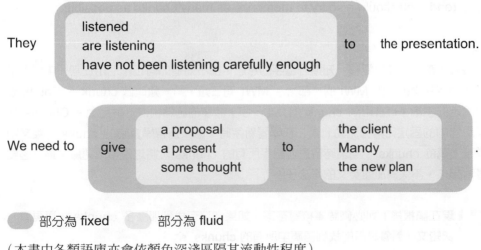

They　| listened / are listening / have not been listening carefully enough | to　| the presentation.

We need to　| give | a proposal / a present / some thought | to | the client / Mandy / the new plan | .

　　部分為 fixed　　　　部分為 fluid

（本書中各類語庫亦會依顏色深淺區隔其流動性程度）

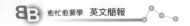

相信各位能夠舉一反三，想出更多例子。當然， give sth. to sb. 也可寫成 give sb. sth.，但這是另外一個 chunk 了。同樣是固定和流動的元素兼具。希望各位能看得出來。

Chunks 通常是短的，包括 meaning words（意義字，如 listen 、 depend）加 function words（功能字，如 to 、 on）。相信你已經知道的 chunks 很多，但會用的卻很少！我們來做另一個 Task ，看看是不是都懂了。不要先看答案哦！

Task 3

請閱讀下列短文，並將你找出的 chunks 畫底線。

Everyone is familiar with the experience of knowing what a word means, but not knowing how to use it accurately in a sentence. This is because words are nearly always used as part of an MWI. There are three kinds of MWIs. The first is called a chunk. A chunk is a combination of words which is more or less fixed. Every time a word in the chunk is used, it must be used with its partner(s). Chunks combine fixed and fluid elements of language. When you learn a new word, you should learn the chunk. There are thousands of chunks in English. One way you can help yourself to improve your English is by noticing and keeping a database of the chunks you find as you read. You should also try to memorize as many chunks as possible.

【中譯】

每個人都有這樣的經驗：知道一個字的意思，卻不知道如何正確地用在句子中。這是因為每個字都必須當作 MWI 的一部分。 MWI 有三類，第一類叫做 chunk 。 Chunk 幾乎是固定的字串，每當用到 chunk 的其中一字，該字的詞夥也得一併用上。 Chunks 包含了語言中的固定元素和流動元素。在學習新字時，應該連帶學會它的 chunk 。英文中有成千上萬的 chunks 。閱讀時留意並記下所有的 chunks ，將之彙整成語庫，最好還要盡量背起來，不失為加強英文的好法子。

答案 現在請根據下列必備語庫核對答案，如果你沒有找到那麼多 chunks ，可再看一次短文，看看是否能找到語庫中所有的 chunks 。

簡報必備語庫　前言 1

- ... be familiar with n.p. ...
- ... experience of Ving ...
- ... how to V ...
- ... be used as n.p. ...
- ... part of n.p. ...
- ... there are ...
- ... kinds of n.p. ...
- ... the first ...
- ... be called n.p. ...
- ... a combination of n.p. ...
- ... more or less ...

- ... every time + n. clause
- ... be used with n.p. ...
- ... combine sth. and sth. ...
- ... elements of n.p. ...
- ... thousands of n.p. ...
- ... in English ...
- ... help yourself to V ...
- ... keep a database of n.p. ...
- ... try to V ...
- ... as many as ...
- ... as many as possible ...

★ 📂 語庫小叮嚀

◆ 注意，上面語庫中的 chunks，be 動詞以原形 be 表示，而非 is、was、are 或 were。

◆ 記下 chunks 時，前後都加上 …（刪節號）。

◆ 注意，有些 chunks 後面接的是 V（go、write 等原形動詞）或 Ving（going、writing 等），有的則接 n.p.（noun phrase，名詞片語）或 n. clause（名詞子句）。我於「本書使用說明」中會對此詳細說明。

　　好，現在我們要看的是第二類 MWI：set-phrases。Set-phrases 比 chunks 固定。通常字串較長，可能是由幾個 chunks 構成的。Set-phrases 通常包含句子的句首或句尾，甚至兩者兼具，這表示有時一個完整的句子也是一種 set-phrase。Chunks 通常是沒頭沒尾的片段文字組合。Set-phrases 在架構簡報用語時非常常見。現在請參考以下的必備語庫，並做 Task。

Task 4

看看下列語庫中簡報常用的 set-phrases，勾選你認識的 set-phrases。

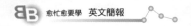
簡報必備語庫　前言 2

- As you can see, ...
- Going on to n.p. ...
- I'd like to draw your attention to n.p. ...
- I'd like to draw your attention to the fact that + n. clause
- I'd now like you to look at n.p. ...
- If you look at this (chart / graph / table), you can see n.p. ...
- If you look at this (chart / graph / table), you can see that + n. clause
- If you look here you can see n.p. ...
- If you look here you can see that + n. clause
- It is clear from this (chart / graph / table / movement) that + n. clause

語庫小叮嚀

◆ 因為 set-phrases 是三大類中最固定的，各位在學習時，得特別注意 set-phrases 的每個細節。我稍後會進一步講解。

◆ 請注意有些 set-phrases 是以 n.p. 結尾；有些則是以 n. clause 結尾。稍後再詳細解說。

　　學習 set-phrases 的好處是，在使用的時候無須考慮到文法：你只要把這些用語當作固定字串背起來，原原本本照用即可。本書大部分的 Task 都與 set-phrases 有關，所以我在下一節中會對此加強解說。現在，讓我們先來看看第三大類 MWI ： word partnerships 。

　　Word partnerships 是這三類字串中流動性最高的。其中包含兩個以上的意義字（不同於 chunks 含意義字和功能字），通常是「動詞＋形容詞＋名詞」，或「名詞＋名詞」的組合。各行各業用的 chunks 和 set-phrases 都一樣，但不同產業用的 word partnerships 就不同了。例如，如果你是在製藥業服務，那你所需的 word partnerships 則和資訊業的人士不同。做完下面的 Task ，你就會明白我的意思。

Task 5

請看下面各組字串，請依據其 word partnerships 判斷各組所代表的產業。見範例 1 。

1.

- government regulations
- drug trial
- patient response
- hospital budget
- key opinion leader
- patent law

產業名稱：　_醫藥界_

2.

- risk assessment
- non-performing loan
- credit rating
- share price index
- low inflation
- bond portfolio

產業名稱：_____

3.

- bill of lading
- shipment details
- customs delay
- shipping date
- letter of credit
- customer service

產業名稱：_____

4.

- latest technology

- user interface
- system problem
- repetitive strain injury
- input data
- installation wizard

產業名稱：_____

答案
2. 銀行與金融業
3. 進出口業
4. 資訊科技業

如果你在上面其中一個產業工作，毫無疑問的，一定早就認出其中的一些 word partnerships 。

現在我們得再度調整對 Leximodel 字串學習法的敘述：

Language consists of words which appear with other words. These combinations can be categorized as chunks, set-phrases and word partnerships and placed along a spectrum of predictability, with fixed combinations at one end, and fluid combinations at the other.
　　語言由字串構成。所有的字串可以分成三大類—— chunks 、 set-phrases 和 word partnerships ，並且可依其可預測的程度區隔，可預測度愈高的一端是固定字串，可預測度愈低的一端是流動字串。

新的 Leximodel 圖示如下：

The Spectrum of Predictability 可預測度

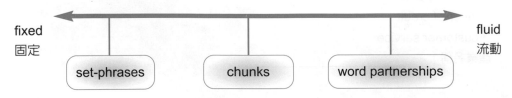

學英文學好 chunks ，文法自然會進步，因為大部分的文法錯誤都源自於寫錯 chunks 。學英文時專攻 set-phrases ，英語功能會加強，因為 set-phrases 都是功能性字串。學英文時在 word partnerships 下功夫，字彙會增加。因此最後的 Leximodel 圖示如下：

The Spectrum of Predictability 可預測度

functions		grammar		vocabulary

fixed
固定

fluid
流動

set-phrases		chunks		word partnerships

Leximodel 的優點在於無論說、寫英文，均無須為文法規則傷透腦筋。學英文時首重建立 chunks 、 set-phrases 和 word partnerships 語庫，多學多益，你再也不必勞心費神學文法，或者苦苦思索如何在文法中套入單字。這三類 MWI 用來輕而易舉，而且更符合人腦記憶和使用語言的習慣。本節結束前，請做一個 Task ，確定你對 Leximodel 已經完全了解，同時驗證這方法確實簡單好用。現在請做下面的 Task ，記住，做完後再看語庫。

Task 6

 Track 前言 1

請看以下的簡報片段及其中譯。然後將 chunks 、 set-phrases 與 word partnerships 畫上不同顏色的底線，最後完成下表。見範例。

OK. This graph displays the sales figures for the last quarter of this year compared with the figures for the last quarter of last year. We can see from the graph that this year's figures are much lower than the previous year's. Let me remind you, however, that these figures are not quite complete. This is because we are still waiting for the results from a sales person who has been on leave. In general, these figures suggest that results this year are going to be comparable to results from last year. Let's turn now to costs, which we can see here.

13

【中譯】

　　好。這張圖呈現的是今年與去年最後一季銷售數字的比較。我們從本圖可看到，今年的數字要比去年同季低得多。這是因為我們還在等一位休假中的業務同仁提供某些數據，所以這些數字並不十分完整。然而，這些數字顯示今年的業績和去年相當。現在讓我們來看成本的部分，在這邊。

Set-phrases	Chunks	Word Partnerships
• This graph displays ...	• ... compared with ...	• sales figures

答案 ▌請以下列的必備語庫來核對答案。

簡報必備語庫　前言 3

Set-phrases	Chunks	Word Partnerships
• This graph displays ...	• ... compared with ...	• sales figures
• We can see from this graph that ...	• ... the last quarter of ...	• this year
• Let me remind you that ...	• ... are much lower than ...	• last year
• This is because ...	• ... the same ...	• the previous year
• In general ...	• ... waiting for ...	• sales person
• These figures suggest that ...	• ... results from ...	
• Let's turn now to ...	• ... been on leave ...	
• ... which we can see here.	• ... are going to be ...	
	• ... be comparable to ...	

★ 📁 語庫小叮嚀

◆ 注意，set-phrases 通常是以大寫開頭，或以句點結尾。三點（…）表示句子的流動部分。

◆ 注意，chunks 的開頭和結束都是三個點，表示 chunks 大部分為句子的中間部分。

◆ 注意，word partnerships 都至少包含兩個意義字。

　　如果你的答案不如參考答案完整，別擔心，要能找出一篇文章中所有的固定元素，需要多加練習才行。但是我保證一旦你能找出像參考答案一樣多的 MWI，那就表示你的英文已經差不多達到登峰造極的境界了！很快你便能擁有這樣的能力。本書結束前，我會請你再做一次這個 Task，讓你自行判斷學習成果。現在有時間的話，建議你找一篇英文文章，英文為母語的人寫的電子郵件，或者雜誌或網路上的文章皆可，請用該篇文章做相同的練習。熟能生巧哦！

本書使用說明

進行到此，我猜你大概心裡覺得 Leximodel 的概念好像不錯，但腹中仍有疑問吧？這樣吧，我來看看是否能夠為你解答。

我該如何實際運用 Leximodel 學英文？為什麼 Leximodel 和我以前碰到的英文教學法截然不同？

簡而言之，我的答案是：只要知道字詞的組合和這些組合的固定程度，就能簡化英語學習的過程，同時大幅減少犯錯的機率。

以前的教學法教你學好文法，然後套用句子，邊寫邊造句。用這方法寫作不僅有如牛步，而且稍不小心便錯誤百出，想必你早就有切身的體驗。現在只要用 Leximodel 建立 chunks、set-phrases 和 word partnerships 語庫，接著只需背起來就能學會英文寫作了。

這本書如何以 Leximodel 教學？

本書告訴你如何學習和運用簡報中最常出現的固定組合（chunks、set-phrases 和 word partnerships，不過大多數是 set-phrases）。並教你如何每天留意並記下所看到的英文，幫你增強英文基礎。

為什麼要留意字串中所有的字，很重要嗎？

不知道何故，大多數人對眼前的英文視而不見，分明擺在面前仍然視若無睹。他們緊盯著字詞的意思，卻忽略了傳達字詞意思的方法。每天瀏覽的固定 MWI 多不勝數，只不過你沒有發覺這些 MWI 是固定、反覆出現的字串罷了。任何語言都有這種現象。這樣吧，我們來做個實驗，你就知道我說的是真是假。請做下面的 Task。

Task 7

看看以下的 set-phrases，並選出正確的。

- Regarding the report you sent me ...
- Regarding to the report you sent me ...

- Regards to the report you sent me ...
- With regards the report you sent ...
- To regard the report you sent me ...
- Regard to the report you sent me ...

　　不論你選的是哪個，我敢說你們一定覺得這題很難。你可能每天都看到這個 set-phrase，可是卻從來沒有仔細留意當中的每一個字（**其實第一個 set-phrase 是正確答案，其餘都是錯的！**）。這就證明了我在教 set-phrase 時提到的第一個告誡沒錯。無論如何，一定要加強注意所接觸到的文字，但絕對只能選擇以英文為母語的人為仿效對象。所謂「英文為母語的人士」，我指的是有受過教育的美國人、英國人、澳洲人、紐西蘭人、加拿大人或南非人，但不一定是白人。如果英文非母語，就算是老闆也不可完全信任。公司中若有人在十年前到美國念過博士，英文能力公認好得沒話說，也信不過。要特別注意：有部分英文為母語的人士的英文很不可靠，就如同很多國人的中文很不可靠一樣。所以你起碼要選擇受過高等教育的母語人士，或已經建立品牌的英文出版物。

　　如果多留意每天接觸到的固定字串，久而久之一定會記起來，轉化成自己英文基礎的一部分，這可是諸多文獻可考的事實。刻意注意閱讀時遇到的 MWI，亦可增加學習效率。 Leximodel 正能幫你達到這一點。

需要小心哪些問題？

　　本書中許多 Task 的目的，即在於幫你克服學 set-phrases 時遇到的問題。學 set-phrases 的要領在於：務必留意 set-phrases 中所有的字。

　　從 Task 7 中，你已發現其實自己不如想像中那麼細心注意 set-phrases 中所有的字。接下來我要更確切地告訴你學 set-phrases 時的注意事項，這對學習非常重要，請勿草率閱讀。學習和使用 set-phrases 時，需要注意的細節有三大類：

1. **短字**（如 a、the、to、in、at、on 和 but）。這些字很難記，但是瞭解了這點，即可以說是跨出一大步了。 Set-phrases 極為固定，用錯一個短字，整個 set-phrase 都會改變，等於是寫錯了。
2. **字尾**（有些字的字尾是 -ed，有些是 -ing，有些是 -ment，有些是 -s，或者沒有 -s）。字尾改變了，字的意思也會隨之改變。 Set-phrase 極為固定，寫錯其

中一字的字尾，整個 set-phrase 都會改變，等於是寫錯了。

3. **Set-phrase 的結尾**（有的 set-phrase 以 n. clause 結尾，有的以 n.p. 結尾，有的以 V 結尾，有的以 Ving 結尾），我們稱之為 code 。許多人犯錯，問題即出在句子中 set-phrase 與其他部分的銜接之處。學習 set-phrase 時，必須將 code 當作 set-phrase 的一部分一併背起來。 Set-phrase 極為固定， code 寫錯，整個 set-phrase 都會改變，等於是寫錯了。

教學到此，請再做一個 Task ，確定你能夠掌握 code 的用法。

Task 8

請看以下 code 的定義，然後依表格將字串分門別類。第一個字串已先替你找到它的位置了。

n. clause = noun clause（名詞子句）。 n. clause 一定包含主詞和動詞。例如： I need your help. 、 She is on leave. 、 We are closing the department. 、 What is your estimate? 等。

n.p. = noun phrase（名詞片語），這其實就是 word partnership ，只是不含動詞或主詞。例如： financial news 、 cost reduction 、 media review data 、 joint stock company 等。

V = verb（動詞）。

Ving = verb ending in -ing（以 -ing 結尾的動詞）。以前你的老師可能稱之為**動名詞**。

- ~~bill of lading~~
- customer complaint
- decide
- did you remember
- do
- doing
- go
- great presentation
- having
- he is not
- help
- I'm having a meeting
- John wants to see you
- knowing
- look after
- our market share
- your new client
- see
- sending
- talking
- we need some more data
- wrong figures

- helping
- you may remember

n. clause	n.p.	V	Ving
	• bill of lading		

答案 ▍請以下列語庫核對答案。

簡報必備語庫　前言 3

n. clause	n.p.	V	Ving
• you may remember • we need some more data • did you remember • John wants to see you • I'm having a meeting • he is not	• wrong figures • customer complaint • bill of lading • our market share • your new client • great presentation	• help • do • see • look after • decide • go	• helping • knowing • doing • having • sending • talking

★ 🗂 語庫小叮嚀

◆ 注意，n. clause 的 verb 前面一定要有主詞。

◆ 注意，noun phrase 基本上即為 word partnership。

　　總而言之，學習 set-phrases 時容易出錯的主要問題如下：

1. 短字
2. 字尾

3. Set-phrases 的結尾

這不會太困難，不是嗎？

如果沒有文法規則可循，我怎麼知道自己的 set-phrases 用法正確無誤？

閱讀要比說容易。說話時你需要仰賴自己的記憶，所以或許有點困難。然而，本書納入兩大工具，協助各位簡化這個過程。

1. **學習目標記錄表**：本書的附錄四中有一份「學習目標記錄表」。各位開始進行本書的各個 Task 之前，應將記錄表多印幾份。因為 set-phrases 數量頗多，可以選擇幾個來作重點學習。利用記錄表，將每個章節的必備語庫中想要學習的用語記下來。我建議每個禮拜記錄 10 個用語。

2. **CD**：清晰的發音是簡報成功的關鍵之一，本書非常強調發音，因此各位將會一直借助 CD，這不但對發音有益，也有助於提昇聽力，並讓你們的學習更有趣、更有效。利用 CD 來練習你挑出並寫在記錄表上的 set-phrases，每天花 10 分鐘來聆聽與複誦，會比禮拜天晚上花 2 個小時還有效。

與其擔心出錯，以及該用或違反哪些文法規則，不如參照本書語庫裡的用語以及 CD 裡的內容，熟能生巧。現在請做下面的 Task，不要先看答案。

Task 9　　　　　　　　　　　　　Track 前言 2

請聽「Track 前言 2」，然後在題號後寫下你聽到的內容。

1. _____
2. _____
3. _____
4. _____
5. _____

答案

1. This graph display the sales figures for the last quarter ...
2. We could see from this graph that this year's figures are much lower than the previous year's.
3. This is because of we are still waiting for some results.

4. These figures suggest that comparable results.

5. Let's turn now to see the costs here.

你可能會覺得這些句子有些怪，別急，請繼續做下一個 Task 。

Task 10

請將「簡報必備語庫　前言 3」裡的 set-phrases 和上題的答案作比較。你能看出 CD 中的句子和語庫中的有什麼不同嗎？請寫出正確的句子和錯誤原因的編號（1. 短字； 2. 字尾； 3. set-phrases 的結尾）。見範例。

1. This graph display the sales figures for the last quarter ...

   This graph displays the sales figures for the last quarter. (2)

2. We could see from this graph that this year's figures are much lower than the previous year's.

3. This is because of we are still waiting for some results.

4. These figures suggest that comparable results.

5. Let's turn now to see the costs here.

 2. We can see from this graph that this year's figures are much lower than the previous year's. (1)

3. This is because we are still waiting for some results. (1)

4. These figures suggest that the results are comparable. (3)

5. Let's turn now to the costs. (3)

　　如果你的答案和上列的南轅北轍，請再回頭看看本節，特別注意 Task 8 和對於 set-phrases 細節三個問題的解說。你也可以再讀、聽 Task 6 的簡報片段（Track 前言 1），看看其中的 set-phrases 是如何運用的。

　　本書有許多 Task 會幫各位將注意力集中在 set-phrases 的細節上，你只須作答和核對答案，無須擔心背後原因。

本書的架構為何？

　　本書分為三個部分。第一個部分是簡報的引言、簡報的原則、以及簡報引言的實用用語、和清晰的發音。第二部分則是簡報的主體。這個部分會告訴各位準備、操練、演出的程序，以及簡報主體常用的用語。還有視覺資料的設計與運用。第三部分介紹的是簡報總結的用語，以及如何應對問答。

　　每個章節大致分為兩部分：第一部分說明用語，第二個部分「實戰要領」則對準備、練習、或進行簡報的技巧提供實際的建議。

　　現在請花幾分鐘的時間看看目錄，熟悉接下來的章節。

　　本書介紹的用語大都是 set-phrases 的形式，因為即使簡報的主題不同，用語大致一樣。我不知道各位的簡報主題，所以對於簡報的內容無法幫上忙，這部分你得自己負責。但各位常用的 word partnerships 我會提供建議。這些用語會在每個章節的「簡報必備語庫」以及 CD 中出現，供各位仿效、學習。善用 CD 對各位的學習是很重要的。書末附錄一提供了各章節「簡報必備語庫」一覽表，方便各位使用。

我如何充分利用本書？

　　在此有些自習的建議，協助各位獲致最大的學習效果。

1. 請逐章逐節看完本書。為了提供更多記憶 set-phrases 的機會，本書會反覆提到一些語言和概念，因此倘若一開始有不解之處，請耐心看下去，多半念到本書後面的章節時自然就會恍然大悟。
2. 如果在讀本書的期間有機會聆聽簡報，試著聽聽簡報中的用語、思考你從本書學得的概念。
3. 每個 Task 都要做。這些 Task 有助於記憶本書中的字串，亦可加強你對這些字

串的理解，不可忽視。

4. 建議你用鉛筆做 Task 。如此寫錯了還可以擦掉再試一次。

5. 做分類 Task 時（請見第二章 Task 2.2），在每個 set-phrase 旁做記號或寫下號碼即可。但是建議有空時，還是將 set-phrases 抄在正確的一欄中。還記得當初是怎麼學中文的嗎？抄寫能夠加深印象！

6. 利用書末附錄四「學習目標記錄表」追蹤自己的進步，並挑選自己要用在簡報中的用語。選擇的時候，不妨記住以下重點：
   • 選擇困難、奇怪、或新的用語。
   • 如果可以的話，避免使用你已經知道、或覺得自在的用語。
   • 特意運用這些新的用語。

7. 如果你下定決心要進步，建議你和同事組成 K 書會，一同閱讀和做 Task 。

在研讀本書之前，還有哪些須知？

Yes, You can do it!

翻開第一章前，請回到引言的「學習目標」，勾出自認為達成的項目。希望全部都能夠打勾，如果沒有，請重新閱讀相關段落。

祝學習有成！

PART 1
簡報的引言

UNIT 1

關於簡報的重要事項

achieving
success

引言與學習目標

很多人在做英文簡報時，會套用中文簡報的技巧和程序。他們覺得既然中文簡報可行，英文簡報一定也行得通。不過，跟做中文簡報比起來，他們的英文簡報很可能會遜色很多。這是因為在做英文簡報的過程中，他們忽略了簡報成功的最重要因素：**簡報者所使用的語言**。中文為母語者在做中文簡報時，他們無須顧慮語言的問題，因為沒有這個必要。但是遇到英文簡報，他們就必須有所顧慮了。在進行英文簡報的過程中，如果忽略這個重要的因素，可能導致簡報的說明不清、難以了解，結果乏味無趣。

無趣 —— 成功簡報的頭號大敵！

在「前言」中我已經提過，本書的目的是在教授各位簡報用語。但我同時也會提供一些技巧與程序，希望各位的英文簡報能獲得更佳的結果。這個章節中，我將介紹進行英文簡報的四個關鍵概念，希望各位在閱讀本書、以及實際進行英文簡報時能夠謹記這幾個觀念。

本章節結束時，你應該達到的學習目標如下：

☐ 了解簡報的目的
☐ 了解具備個人目的的重要性
☐ 了解「5 Ks」
☐ 了解「3 Tells」
☐ 了解「3 Ps」
☐ 了解一些應付常見的臨場焦慮（performance anxieties）的建議。

一開始我想請大家做個 Task ，在一張紙上、或你的筆記本裡以中文或英文寫下你的答案。

Task 1.1

以一個句子描述，依你之見，簡報的目的是什麼？

答案
- 我想，你可能會寫：「簡報的目的就是提供資訊」或是「簡報的目的是在溝通。」大多數人都把簡報視為傳達訊息的機會。
- 如果你是這樣寫的，那很好。如果你寫了不同的意見，那麼請繼續看下去。

　　雖然大多數的人都認為簡報就是傳達某些訊息的機會，但這並不完全正確，因為這樣的定義太過廣泛而不實用。想想看，如果只是為了傳達某些訊息，那麼簡報和電子郵件又有什麼差別？電子郵件也可以傳遞訊息。而且如果你把要說的都寫在郵件裡頭，然後發出去，大家都可省去聚在一起聽簡報的時間。（我想你在聽簡報時一定常常有這個想法：「看電子郵件不就行了嗎？還可以省下一堆時間！」）

　　你也許會說電子郵件是書寫的形式，簡報則是口語的溝通。沒錯，但是如果把簡報和其他形式的口語溝通做比較，結果會如何？

Task 1.2

簡報、演說、及授課的目的有何不同，想想看，並將答案寫下來。

答案
- 它們都是口語溝通的形式，由一人對一群人講述。
- 演說的目的通常是在促進社會和諧（facilitate social harmony）。想想看婚禮、退休歡送會、慶生會、歡迎會等場合的演說。
- 授課的目的是在傳授學理知識（impart academic knowledge）。這種場合的焦點在於授課的內容，以及如何傳授知識。
- 簡報的目的有許多相似處，但還是有很多不同。做簡報的目的是為了完成商業交易（complete a business transaction）。這一點是我提出的第一個關鍵概念。

四個簡報的關鍵概念

關鍵概念 1

The purpose of a presentation is to complete a business transaction.
做簡報的目的是為了完成商業交易。

　　這個關鍵概念非常重要。進行簡報的時候，你應該清楚自己的目的是什麼，也就是說，你希望完成什麼樣的商業交易。我們來做另一個 Task ，以確保你了解我的意思。

Task 1.3

配合題，請將左欄的動詞與右欄的名詞配對，組成 word partnerships ，用以描述簡報最終所希望達成的商業交易。每題答案可能不只一個。

_____ **1.** ask for	a) a budget	
_____ **2.** deliver	b) a client	
_____ **3.** describe and explain	c) a price increase	
_____ **4.** get	d) a proposal	
_____ **5.** justify	e) marketing strategy	
_____ **6.** make	f) project status	
_____ **7.** review	g) a product	
_____ **8.** sell	h) support for a project	
_____ **9.** show	i) your business skills	
	j) your presentation skills	
	k) results	

答案
1. acdhk **2.** dk **3.** acdgk **4.** abcdghk **5.** acdgh
6. ad **7.** acdgh **8.** acg **9.** gh

- 希望各位能看出來，簡報的目的應該非常具體，並且是能夠達成的。設定無法達成的目的不是明智之舉，例如， get instant promotion「立刻獲得升遷」！
- 你的目的愈具體，在簡報全程對你的幫助就愈大。

　　簡報之所以不同於其他形式的商業溝通（不論書寫或口語形式）的另一個原因是，簡報是（或應該是）一個活動（an event）。每一種活動都有某些要素需要由活動管理人（event manager）來管理。以簡報來說，活動管理人（event manager）就是你，而活動的要素：就是你的目的、你的資料、以及你的觀眾。接下來，讓我們來探討「the 5Ks」這個關鍵概念。

關鍵概念 2

The 5 Ks:

- **K**now your purpose
  確定目的
- **K**now your audience
  了解觀眾
- **K**now your material
  熟悉內容
- **K**eep it short
  儘量簡短
- **K**eep it simple
  化繁為簡

　　我們來仔細看看「the 5Ks」是怎麼回事。

Know your purpose
確定目的
　　我想各位一定已經了解這一點了。在簡報的規劃與實踐等各個階段都必須謹記自己的目的。這有助你將焦點鎖定在重要的事情上。你在任何階段的目標都應該是「達成目的」。

Know your audience
了解觀眾

你的觀眾攸關你該使用哪一種風格的語言。如果你的觀眾包括客戶、你的上司、或是公司董事，你就得使用比較正式的用語。如果對象是同事或者較資淺的同仁，你的用語就無須這麼正式。在簡報的規劃階段，了解簡報對象以及他們對簡報的期望是很重要的，因為這樣有助於設計適合的簡報——究竟應該正式或非正式。了解簡報對象將有助你達成目的。本書的 Task 中有許多 set-phrases，各位在面對不同類型的觀眾時可以選擇使用。

Know your material
熟悉內容

專業的簡報人員會非常清楚下一步要做什麼、下一張投影片是什麼內容、重要數據，並且能夠清楚地解釋各項要點。做簡報卻無法清楚掌握自己的材料是說不過去的，這顯示了你事前沒有做好準備。如果不了解自己的材料，就很難達成簡報的目的。了解材料也包括如何操作設備，以及你進行簡報的場地。在第四章中，我將談到如何有效地準備材料。

Keep it short
盡量簡短

這是個事實——我想你一定也有同感——許多簡報都太過冗長。簡報進行太久，簡報的觀眾會感到不耐煩，結果，你也無法達成目的。因此在設計簡報時，一定要記住這點。選擇能夠幫助你達到目的的資訊就夠了。第五章中會有更詳細的說明。

Keep it simple
化繁為簡

聽取資訊要比閱讀資訊困難多了——特別是如果你的簡報對象和你一樣，都不是以英文為母語。所以，你得使用簡單、直截了當的用語來表達，你所提供的視覺畫面也務求簡潔。採用簡單明瞭的方式可有助你達成目的。第五章中會有更詳細的說明。

我剛才提過，聽取資訊要比讀取困難得多。但是如果你知道這些資訊的架構，在聆聽時能夠在腦中建立類似的架構，要了解和記住這些訊息會比較容易。因此，所有的簡報都得規劃為三個部分。接著就來談談下一個關鍵概念。

關鍵概念 3

The 3 Tells:

- **Tell** them what you are going to tell them.
  告知觀眾你將報告的內容
- **Tell** them.
  告知觀眾內容
- **Tell** them what you've told them.
  告知觀眾你已經報告過的內容

接著來說明這「3 Tells」。

Tell them what you are going to tell them.
告知觀眾你將報告的內容

如果人們預先知道接下來的架構，那麼在聆聽簡報的時候會比較容易記住這些內容。所以，你得事先說明簡報的架構，然後再開始介紹你準備的訊息。我們稱之為簡報的引言（opening section），接下來第二、三章都是和引言有關。

Tell them.
告知觀眾內容

在說明資訊架構之後，才真正進入簡報內容的部分。由於大家已經先被預告了簡報架構，因此會比較容易記住簡報的資訊，而你的目的也就比較容易達成。這個部分我們稱之為主體（body section），第四至第七章中會對此加以說明。

Tell them what you've told them.
告知觀眾你已經報告過的內容

研究顯示人們對於聽過三遍的事情會牢記在心。這就是為什麼當簡報的主體部分結束後，你還得再進行一個總結（closing section），將方才報告的內容做一個摘要，並再次清楚地重複你的要點。大多數人不會記得你在主體部分講了些什麼，不過他們通常都會記住引言和總結的部分。第八和第九章將會介紹如何做一個具有震撼力的總結。

好了，到目前為止的說明都蠻理論的，希望沒讓各位覺得乏味。接下來我要介紹簡報過程中比較實用的部分，同時也請各位回想一下自己實際的經驗。

Task 1.4

列出一些你在做英文簡報時會遭遇的問題，列出愈多愈好。

答案
- 我無法提供一個制式的答案，因為每個人都有不同的問題。不過，請各位妥善保管這張清單，因為在本書結束時，我會請你們把清單再拿出來，看看本書對各位是否有所助益。
- 我希望各位不要只注意簡報實際報告的部分，規劃與執行簡報的全部過程都應該被考慮到。

現在來看看第四個關鍵概念──The 3 Ps。

關鍵概念 4

The 3 Ps:
- **P**repare
  準備
- **P**ractice
  操練
- **P**erform
  演出

要成功地用英文做簡報，有一點很重要，就是不要只考慮到站在台上發表簡報的部分，而是應該全程關照，從準備到發表階段都要面面俱到。現在來仔細看看每個環節。

Prepare
準備

這個階段包括設定簡報的目的、進行背景研究、收集資料、思考如何組織簡報的架構、設計投影片與講義、以及安排場地和設備。英文簡報在準備階段需要的程序和

技術和中文簡報有所不同。在第四和第五章中，會有針對「準備階段」的小叮嚀與建議。

Practice
操練

　　在英文簡報的過程中，練習階段常常會被省略或是草草帶過。可是在我看來，這是最重要的部分。在這個階段應該好好練習發音，以便清楚地表達關鍵內容的 word partnerships 和 set-phrases；並組織材料的順序，這樣自己才知道接下來要說些什麼；而且還要練習語氣、手勢和姿態，以及熟悉設備的使用。好的簡報應該進行得平順、專業，是好幾個小時練習的成果。在本書的第二和第三章有針對「操練階段」的小叮嚀和建議。

Perform
演出

　　簡報人員的職責就是說服觀眾，讓他們相信你、你的產品、或你的看法。你得協助觀眾建立對你、以及對你簡報專業能力的信心。如果觀眾對你簡報的能力沒有信心，對你的產品或是看法也不會有信心。你的簡報也就宣告失敗了。我在前面的關鍵概念中提到簡報是一種活動，簡報也是一種表演，而你就是主演的明星！在本章和第五、六章中，會有針對「演出階段」的小叮嚀和建議。

Task 1.5

花點時間想一想，你花在每個階段的時間各佔多少比例。

答案 │ 若要進行真正有效的英文簡報，我會建議各位花在每個 P 的時間比例如下圖所示。你可以看出花在練習上的時間比例，比其他兩項的總合還要多。你目前籌備簡報的方式和這個圖表有多接近呢？

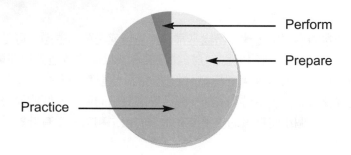

實戰要領：克服臨場焦慮

在這個部分我要談談，一般人在從事表演或任何種類的演說時普遍會有的恐懼和憂慮。我們稱之為常見的臨場焦慮（common performance anxieties）。

Task 1.6

請看下表所列的臨場焦慮，如果你的簡報經驗中，曾在某些階段出現過以下現象，請在旁邊打勾。

( ) 我不知道該怎麼站。
( ) 我不知道該看哪裡。
( ) 我不知道兩隻手該做什麼。
( ) 我覺得很緊張。
( ) 我討厭成為注目的焦點。
( ) 我的聲音不夠大。
( ) 我今天的頭髮亂得一團糟；真希望我不是穿這套衣服。
( ) 如果忘了接下來該做什麼，怎麼辦？
( ) 如果出錯了，怎麼辦？
( ) 觀眾是不是在笑我？

答案 即使是經驗豐富的簡報人員、演說家，或是演員，也會有這類的焦慮感，知道這點可能會讓你比較舒坦些，因為你不是孤單的。請看下面的說明，看看我對應付這類恐懼的建議。希望能對各位有幫助！

我不知道該怎麼站。

當你站在一群人面前，會覺得不自在，而且還不知道該怎麼站，這些都是很普遍的感受。應該把重心放在兩腳呢？還是一腳就好了？應不應該靠著桌子呢？兩手該不該交叉？我相信各位一定都經歷過這些感覺。

不過，你得記住一個很重要的觀念：你對自我的認知和觀眾對你的認知之間是有

差距的。比方說，觀眾並不認為你看起來有什麼不對勁，他們也不知道你覺得不自在。所以，沒有必要將自己的感覺投射到觀眾身上。

抬頭挺胸，但不要僵硬。挺起胸膛可以讓自己有信心，重心平均放在兩腳可以感覺比較踏實。

我不知道兩隻手該做什麼。

記住，聽簡報的人並不會像你一樣注意你的雙手。

不妨試試拿枝筆或指示棒子在手上，另一隻手則插進口袋。你也可以用手勢來強調某些論點。在鏡子前練習手勢的運用。第六章中有一些圖片，可供你參考。

我不知道該看哪裡。

簡報的觀眾看的是你，所以看他們就好了！試著在整個簡報過程中，和每個觀眾至少有一次的目光接觸。別忘了微笑！

我覺得很緊張。

你當然會緊張囉。不過你緊繃的神經同時也幫助你集中精神。記住你的目的，還有最重要的一點，別忘了怎麼呼吸。許多經驗不足的簡報人員之所以緊張，是因為他們的呼吸變得不協調。記住，自然地呼吸。

我討厭成為注目的焦點。

既然身為簡報人員，你就得假裝喜歡大家的目光！如果你很害羞，那就假裝自己一點都不怕。有的時候，如果我覺得靦腆，我會假裝自己是某個酷哥，像是喬治克隆尼，或是約翰屈伏塔。這樣我很快就能放輕鬆，而且能做回我自己。

我的聲音不夠大。

那麼就說大聲點。每個人都有能力發出極大的音量。想想看嬰兒扯著嗓門哭嚎和受過訓練的歌劇演員吧。如果你的聲音很小，那是因為你沒顧及你的觀眾。他們必須聽得到你才行。好好地呼吸，挺起胸膛，記住你的目的，大聲說出來！

我今天的頭髮亂得一團糟；真希望我不是穿這套衣服。

進行簡報的時候，你的穿著只需比觀眾多修飾一點即可。衣著力求簡單正式，這

樣才不會分散觀眾的注意力，而忽略了你或簡報的內容。應該穿著深色，沒有圖案的衣服。如果你是女性，不要戴懸掛式的耳環，因爲這類耳環容易分散觀眾的注意力。如果你是男性，不要繫鮮豔的領帶。如果你會擔心你的頭髮，記住觀眾不會注意它就好了！

如果忘了接下來該做什麼，怎麼辦？

那就暫停一下，看一下你的筆記，然後再繼續。這可不是考試，你是掌控全場的人。讓這個狀況看起來好像是你故意停頓一會兒，好讓觀眾有時間思考你剛剛說的話。記住，觀眾並不知道你忘了要做什麼！所以假裝你什麼都沒忘記吧！

如果出錯了，怎麼辦？

再修正就好了。千萬不要說 sorry ，這一點非常重要。進行簡報的時候，唯一應該道歉的狀況是設備不能正常運作。但如果你咳嗽，或出錯了，或者在說重要的詞句時吃螺絲，千萬不要道歉。如果你道歉，觀眾很難對你產生信心，而且也會打斷簡報的連貫性。

觀眾是不是在笑我？

不是。他們笑是因爲你的笑話，而且觀眾對你簡報的內容比較有興趣，而不是你本身！

好啦，希望你現在覺得舒坦一點。本書中還有更多這類的小叮嚀。在各位接著學習第二章的用語之前，請回到本章的「學習目標」，看看你達成了多少。

UNIT 2

開場白與目的的陳述

achieving
success

引言與學習目標

引言和總結是簡報中重要的兩個部分。聽眾很有可能只記得引言和總結,而把主體的內容忘掉一大半。因此在引言的時候,你有三項主要的任務:

1. 給觀眾一個好印象。

觀眾會在簡報的頭一分鐘內,對你的簡報能力產生印象。所以引言的流暢、專業就顯得異常重要。要獲得這樣的結果,你得運用語氣、儀態、身體語言、以及吸引眾人注意的能力。

2. 讓觀眾對你的簡報產生信心。

如果觀眾對你的簡報能力沒有信心,就不可能對你銷售的產品、或你傳達的訊息產生信心。他們會在簡報的頭一分鐘就決定對你有沒有信心,所以你根本沒有時間可以暖身。

3. 解釋簡報的架構。

如果觀眾能預先對簡報的架構有所了解,將有助於他們吸收資訊。如果你只是一味地給予資訊,而沒有先告知簡報的架構,觀眾難以在腦中組織這些資訊,也就記不住這些資訊。

這個章節中我們要學如何說出流暢、專業的引言,還有開始進行簡報與介紹簡報架構時的用語。同時還要討論如何改進發音以留下專業的印象。看完本章,你應該達到的學習目標如下:

- ❑ 學會「開場白」與「陳述目的」的 set-phrases。
- ❑ 做些練習,學習如何使用這些 set-phrases。
- ❑ 練習使用連音和加強口說的流暢度。
- ❑ 做一些聽力練習。

開場白

我們先來聽幾個簡報的開場白。

Task 2.1

Track 2.1

請聽 Track 2.1 的簡報開場白。這幾個開場白有什麼共通點？

答案
- 它們的結構相同：以一句開場白歡迎大家，或是介紹主講者與其公司；接著以一句話帶出這場簡報的主題或題目，我們將之稱為「陳述目的」（statement of purpose）句。
- 所有的主講者都用一種強而有力和自信的聲調，在一開始就抓住了觀眾的注意力。

這幾個開場白的用語都蠻固定的，我們可以將這些用語當作 set-phrases 來學習。現在來做下一個 Task，記住，做完之前不要先看答案。

Task 2.2

將這些 set-phrases 分類填入下表。

1. Good morning/afternoon/evening, ladies and gentlemen.
2. I'm going to be showing you n.p.
3. My presentation today is going to cover n.p.
4. Thanks for coming today.
5. It's a pleasure for me to V
6. My presentation today focuses on n.p.
7. Today, I'm going to be reporting on n.p.
8. This afternoon I'd like to tell you about n.p.
9. I'd like to thank everyone for coming.
10. Today we're going to take a look at n.p.
11. My presentation today will deal with n.p.

12. I appreciate everyone's attendance today and hope that you will leave this room with a better understanding of n.p.

13. Hello, everybody. My name is ... and I represent ...

開場白 Openings	陳述目的 Statements of Purpose

答案 ┃ 答案請參看下列的必備語庫 2.1 。

簡報必備語庫 2.1

開場白 Openings	陳述目的 Statements of Purpose
• Good morning/afternoon/evening, ladies and gentlemen. • Thanks for coming today. • It's a pleasure for me to make this presentation to you today. • I'd like to thank everyone for coming. • Hello, everybody. My name is ... and I represent ...	• I'm going to be showing you n.p. • My presentation today is going to cover n.p. • My presentation today focuses on n.p. • Today, I'm going to be reporting on n.p. • This afternoon I'd like to tell you about n.p. • Today we're going to take a look at n.p. • My presentation today will deal with n.p. • I appreciate everyone's attendance today and hope that you will leave this room with a better understanding of n.p.

為了加強這些 set-phrases 的學習，各位不妨回頭看看我在本書「前言」中提到學習和使用 set-phrases 的相關要點。這在此是息息相關的。

接下來，我們來練習發音。首先練習開場白的 set-phrases 。現在就來做下一個 Task 。

Task 2.3

 Track 2.2

請聽 Track 2.2 ，練習開場白 set-phrases 的發音。

答案 | 這個練習至少要花十分鐘來做。練習的時候試著不要看 set-phrases ，要專注在聽力與記憶力上。每個 set-phrase 至少練習五遍，接著再看語庫，選幾個你覺得重要的，然後專心練習直到你有信心為止。

陳述目的

　　這裡所說的「陳述目的（statement of purpose）」指的是簡報的主題或題目，通常會用 word partnerships 來表達。現在請做下一個 Task 。

Task 2.4

Track 2.1

再聽一遍 Track 2.1 ，將你聽到的主題字串記下來，並填入下列空格。請看範例 1 。

簡報片段 1： *the marketing plan*
簡報片段 2：＿＿＿＿＿＿＿＿＿＿＿＿
簡報片段 3：＿＿＿＿＿＿＿＿＿＿＿＿
簡報片段 4：＿＿＿＿＿＿＿＿＿＿＿＿
簡報片段 5：＿＿＿＿＿＿＿＿＿＿＿＿
簡報片段 6：＿＿＿＿＿＿＿＿＿＿＿＿

答案 簡報片段 2： just-in-time management
　　　簡報片段 3： sales results
　　　簡報片段 4： our latest product
　　　簡報片段 5： some recent developments
　　　簡報片段 6： the latest work

　　希望你看出來「主題」通常是以 word partnership 來表達。在設定簡報的主題或題目時，也應該像這樣以 word partnership 來表示，這可以給觀眾極深的印象。第四章還有更多 Task ，讓你練習運用 word partnership 以使簡報更具影響力。

　　接下來，練習陳述目的 set-phrases 的發音。

| Word List |

just-in-time management 零庫存管理

Track 2.3

Task 2.5

請聽 Track 2.3，練習陳述目的 set-phrases 的發音。

答案 ┃ 至少花十分鐘來練習。練習的時候試著不要看 set-phrases，專注在聽力與記憶力。

　　既然已經練習過開場白和陳述目的 set-phrases 的發音，接著就試試將它們串在一起成為一個完整的簡報引言。現在請做 Task 2.6。

Task 2.6

將下表中開場白、陳述目的的 set-phrases，以及主題 word partnerships 串在一起，以完成完整的簡報引言。

開場白	陳述目的	主題 Word Partnerships
• Good morning/afternoon /evening, ladies and gentlemen. • Thanks for coming today. • It's a pleasure for me to make this presentation to you today. • I'd like to thank everyone for coming. • Hello, everybody. My name is... and I represent ...	• I'm going to be showing you n.p. • My presentation today is going to cover ... • My presentation today focuses on ... • Today, I'm going to be reporting on ... • This afternoon I'd like to tell you about ... • Today we're going to take a look at ... • My presentation today will deal with ... • I appreciate everyone's attendance today and hope that you will leave this room with a better understanding of ...	• the marketing plan • just-in-time management • sales results • our latest product • some recent developments • the latest work

答案 答案有很多種排列組合，以下是其中之一。

• It's a pleasure for me to make this presentation to you today. This afternoon I'd like to tell you about our latest product.
今天很高興能夠為各位做簡報。這個下午我想跟各位介紹我們最新的產品。

最後以自己工作上常用的主題 word partnerships 來代換，再練習一遍。

實戰要領：連音

在這部分，我要介紹連音的一些基本特點。本章和下一章的「實戰要領」都著重在口說技巧上。我極力建議各位勤練本書所提供的 set-phrases 發音，因為這樣可以幫助各位在整體上更為流暢，流暢的簡報有助於建立觀眾對你的信心。

連音基本上有四點規則。不過在我加以說明之前，各位必須弄清楚什麼是母音（vowel，a、e、i、o、u）和子音（consonant，…t、p、j等）。在下面的說明中，母音簡稱 V，子音為 C。

連音的基本原則：

> There is often no gap, no short silence, between two words.
> **兩個字中間，通常沒有間斷，沒有沉默。**

也就是說，前面一個字的最後一個音通常會和後面一個字的第一個音相連。講話速度一快，就很自然會出現這個現象。也因為這個緣故，你可能會覺得聽英文為母語的人講話很困難，因為他們在字和字中間沒有停頓，結果兩個獨立的字聽起來卻好像是一個長長的字。

請看這個例子：

Good　　evening, ladies　　and　　gentlemen.
　　no gap　　　　　　　no gap　　no gap

Good 的最後一個音是 C（d），而下一個字 evening 的第一個音是 V（e）。連音的規則就是以上一個字的最後一個音和下一個字的第一個音的四種組合為基礎。

請看這四項規則：　　　　　　　　　　　　　　　　　 Track 2.4

規則 1

_____ word₁ _____ **C** _____ **V** _____ word₂ _____

這個組合當中，C 脫離了第一個字的字尾，而加入第二個字，和第二個字字首的 V 結合，如下：

$$\underline{\hspace{3cm} \text{word}_1 \hspace{1cm}} \times \xrightarrow{\hspace{5cm}} \text{CV} \underline{\hspace{2cm} \text{word}_2 \hspace{2cm}}$$

如果快速又正確地講， good evening 聽起來會是： goo devening 。請聽 Track 2.4 的示範。首先你聽到的是分開來講的兩個字，然後是使用連音的唸法。你聽得出差別嗎？

規則 2

$$\underline{\hspace{3cm} \text{word}_1 \hspace{1cm}} C_1 \hspace{4cm} C_2 \underline{\hspace{1cm} \text{word}_2 \hspace{2cm}}$$

這個組合中，如果兩個 C 並不相同， C_1 不需要明顯地發出聲音，音量小到幾乎聽不到。假如兩個 C 都是一樣的，第一個 C 根本不需發音，如下：

$$\underline{\hspace{3cm} \text{word}_1 \hspace{1cm}} \times \xrightarrow{\hspace{5cm}} C \underline{\hspace{1cm} \text{word}_2 \hspace{2cm}}$$

Recent developments 聽起來會是： recendevelopments ； just-in-time management 聽起來會是 just-in-timemanagement 。請聽 Track 2.4 的示範。你聽得出差別嗎?

規則 3

$$\underline{\hspace{3cm} \text{word}_1 \hspace{1cm}} V \hspace{4cm} C \underline{\hspace{1cm} \text{word}_2 \hspace{2cm}}$$

這是最簡單的一種組合，因為你只須把兩個字連在一起，如下：

$$\underline{\hspace{3cm} \text{word}_1 \hspace{1cm}} V \xrightarrow{\hspace{5cm}} C \underline{\hspace{1cm} \text{word}_2 \hspace{2cm}}$$

... be showing ... 聽起來會是 ... beshowing ... ； a pleasure 聽起來會是 apleasure 。請聽 Track 2.4 的示範。

規則 4

$$\underline{\hspace{3cm} \text{word}_1 \hspace{1cm}} V \hspace{4cm} V \underline{\hspace{1cm} \text{word}_2 \hspace{2cm}}$$

這種組合最難，因為你得在兩個字中間插入一個 C。插入的 C 可能是 y、w 或是 r，視兩邊的母音而定。

... you about ... 結果聽起來會是 ... youwabout ...。請聽 Track 2.4 的示範。

好啦，各位已經知道這四個規則了，現在我們拿一個完整的句子來練習。請做下一個 Task。

Task 2.7

根據上述規則，將下句的空隙連在一起。請參考前三個字的連法。

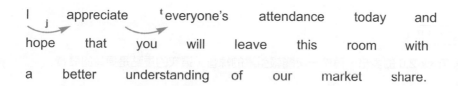

答案
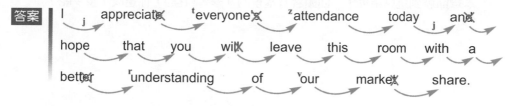

做完這個練習，現在來看看你能否聽得出差別。

Task 2.8

Track 2.5

反覆聽 Track 2.5 的範例。你會聽到同一個句子唸兩次，第一次是每個字分開唸，第二次則是使用連音。聽第二個句子的時候，請依照上面的練習串連字與字間的空隙。

給各位一個良心的建議。如果你覺得有點困惑，或自認為絕對不可能達到那種流

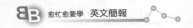

利程度，或者覺得自己實際在講的時候絕對不可能記得這幾個規則——不要擔心！

記住，這些規則只是英文講得比較快時，自然而然會產生的現象。如果覺得困難，只要練習把 set-phrases 講得比你現在的速度快一些即可。**提醒你：連音會使英文簡報更出色，但連得不好會害了簡報，甚至製造負面印象。所以能連則連，沒有把握的話寧可每個字說清楚，不必覺得羞恥。**自己做一些練習吧，以自己最快的速度把 set-phrases 連續唸三遍。

現在你已經了解連音的說話方式，也許你會想回頭再做一遍前面的 Task 。

Task 2.9　　　　　　　　　　　　　　　　　　　 Track 2.2 & 2.3

請再仔細聽一次 Track 2.2 與 2.3 。我們剛才學過連音的特點，你能聽出來嗎？再練習說一遍。

Task 2.10

請回頭看 Task 2.6 的表格，再做一次簡報引言的練習，這次的重點是連音的發音。

本章節就到這兒結束了。回頭看看本章的「學習目標」，你達成了多少呢？

UNIT 3

預告簡報的内容

引言與學習目標

上一章介紹了簡報引言的第一步。在此章節，我要介紹標示用語（signposting），引言的部分也就算完整了。 Signposting 最好的闡釋就是把它想成一本書的目錄。你在考慮買一本書時，可能會先翻到目錄，看看這本書在談些什麼，讓你對書的內容預先有個概念。簡報的 signposting 即是預先告知觀眾簡報的內容和架構。在你進行簡報主體的部分時，有助於觀眾理解、記住你傳達的訊息。這就是我在第一章中提到的「Tell them what you are going to tell them.（告知他們你將報告的內容）」。

在這章中要介紹的是簡報 signposting 的 set-phrases ，並且要做更多的發音練習，這次的重點在音調。本章結束時，你應達成的學習目標如下：

❑ 學到一些有用的 set-phrases ，預告簡報的內容和架構。
❑ 練習發音和這些 set-phrases 。
❑ 學習運用音調。
❑ 練習聽力。
❑ 對「making a move」的意義有些概念，並了解這對簡報結構和簡報的進行有何助益。

預告簡報內容的用語

我們先來做些聽力練習。

Task 3.1  Track 3.1

請聽 Track 3.1 中簡報的引言。它們之間有何共通點？

答案
- 這些引言都有相同的架構：首先，歡迎觀眾或是介紹主講者和公司；接著說明簡報的主題，再來以大綱方式報告簡報要點，最後是結語。
- 所有的主講者都用一種強勢、自信的聲調，從一開始就緊抓住每個人的注意力。

Task 3.2 Track 3.1

請看下列三張簡報主講者所使用的投影片。為投影片挑出 CD 中正確的簡報片段。可以再聽一遍 Track 3.1 。

1.

1. Regional quarterly results
2. Comparison 1: Regional quarterly targets
3. Comparison 2: Regional top performers
4. Comparison 3: Our main competitors
5. Year-end market position

簡報片段 _____

2.

1. Learning English in Taiwan — in overview
2. Competitive advantages for English speakers in the Taiwan labor market
3. Lexikon International: Product range
4. Recommendations

簡報片段 _____

3.

> 1. Current market status
> 2. Threats to market share
> 3. Comparison with Hong Kong
> 4. Five-point strategy for increasing market share

簡報片段 _____

答案
- **1.** 簡報片段 __2__ **2.** 簡報片段 __1__ **3.** 簡報片段 __3__
- 注意，這些投影片和書本的目錄十分相似。投影片上僅有少量的內容，而且都是 word partnerships，不需花費太多時間閱讀。第五章將說明如何設計有影響力的投影片。
- 主講者說明要點時，要點數目不會超過三。例如，簡報片段 2 的主講者並沒有說到 fourthly（第四點）與 fifthly（第五點），而是說 After that ...（在這之後……）以及 When I've done that ...（當我談完這部分……）。

好，現在來看看預告內容與大綱的用語。

Task 3.3

下列為用作標示的 set-phrases，請為它們標出正確的順序，標示簡報第一點者，寫上 F（first）；標示最後一點者，標示 L（last）；中間幾點則寫上 M（middle），將答案寫在下頁的表中。見範例。

1. Second, I plan to discuss n.p. ...

2. I'd then like to conclude with a summary of n.p. ...

3. I'll begin by Ving ...

4. First, I'm going to tell you about n.p. ...

5. At the end (of my presentation), I'll be suggesting that + n. clause

6. Then, I'll move on to V/n.p. ...

7. Next, I'm going to show you n.p. ...

8. Third, I'd like to demonstrate n.p. ...

9. I'm going to start with n.p. ...

10. After that, we'll take a look at n.p. ...

11. Finally, I'll be presenting a summary of n.p. ...

12. I'll begin with n.p. ...

13. For a start, I'm going to bring you up to speed on the current situation.

14. I'm going to present n.p. ...

15. I'd like to open my presentation today by giving you some background information on n.p. ...

16. When I've done that, I'll go on to V ...

17. I'm going to start by Ving ...

第一點（First）

中間的要項（Middle）
Second, I plan to discuss n.p. ...

最後一點（Last）

答案 ▌請以必備語庫 3.1 核對你的答案。

簡報必備語庫 3.1

第一點（First）

- I'll begin by Ving ...
- I'll begin with n.p. ...
- I'm going to start with n.p. ...
- I'm going to start by Ving ...
- First, I'm going to tell you about n.p. ...
- For a start, I'm going to bring you up to speed on the current situation.
- I'd like to open my presentation today by giving you some background information on n.p. ...

中間的要項（Middle）

- Second, I plan to discuss n.p. ...
- Then, I'll move on to V/n.p. ...
- Next, I'm going to show you n.p. ...
- After that, we'll take a look at n.p. ...
- When I've done that, I'll go on to V/n.p. ...
- Third, I'd like to demonstrate n.p. ...

最後一點（Last）

- I'd then like to conclude with n.p. ...
- Finally, I'll be presenting a summary of n.p. ...
- In summary, I'm going to present n.p. ...
- At the end (of my presentation), I'll be suggesting that + n. clause

語庫小叮嚀

◆ 注意 set-phrases 的結尾是 n.p.、V、Ving 或 n. clause，記住這些是很重要的。

好，現在來做些聽力練習。

Task 3.4　 Track 3.1

請聽 Track 3.1 中的簡報片段。一面聽，一面將必備語庫 3.1 中你聽到的 set-phrases 勾起來。

答案 ▎請以書末附錄三的錄音稿檢查答案。檢查的時候，注意 set-phrases 和主講者的其他內容如何連結。

　　接著來練習 set-phrases 的發音。做下一個 Task 時，請回憶上一章中的「連音」規則，試著將你學會的應用到這些新的 set-phrases。

Task3.5　 Track 3.2

請聽 Track 3.2，練習必備語庫 3.1 中 set-phrases 的發音。

答案 ▎至少花 20 分鐘來做這個練習。記住，練習時盡量不要看 set-phrases，專注在聽力和記憶上。每個 set-phrase 都練習至少五遍之後，再看一次所有的 set-phrases，挑選出你想再加強的繼續練習，直到熟練為止。

　　現在來練習使用這些 set-phrases。在下一個 Task 中，建議各位把答案寫在另一張紙上，如此，以後再練習時可以試著使用不同的 set-phrases。

Task3.6

請利用必備語庫 3.1 中的 set-phrases 完成這個簡報。

_____ Ⓐ _____ . Today, _____ Ⓑ _____ last year's results. _____ Ⓒ _____ the results for all regions quarter by quarter. _____ Ⓓ _____ the targets set by the regional office for the year in question, comparing them with the results to give you an idea of our perform-ance. _____ Ⓔ _____ some of the top performers in each region. _____ Ⓕ _____ compare our performance last year with our main competitors' performance over the same period. _____ Ⓖ _____ a summary of our market position at the end of last year.

答案 建議各位大聲朗讀這段簡報，口說練習的方式會比寫答案卷有用得多。因為簡報需要的是口語上的技巧，而非書寫技巧。

記住，練習時必須注意 set-phrase 的結尾，以及 set-phrase 是如何連接句子的其他部分。如果有錄音機，可以把自己的練習錄下來，聽聽看有哪裡需要改進。

接著請核對答案吧！

A
- Good morning/afternoon/evening, ladies and gentlemen
- Thanks for coming today
- It's a pleasure for me to make this presentation to you today
- I'd like to thank everyone for coming
- Hello, everybody. My name is … and I represent …

B
- I'm going to be showing you
- my presentation is going to cover
- my presentation focuses on
- I'm going to be reporting on
- I'd like to tell you about
- we're going to take a look at
- my presentation will deal with

C
- I'll begin with
- I'm going to start with
- First, I'm going to tell you about

D
- Then, I'll move on to
- Next, I'm going to show you
- After that, we'll take a look at
- When I've done that, I'll go on to
- Second, I plan to discuss

E
- Then, I'll move on to
- When I've done that, I'll go on to
- Third, I'd like to demonstrate

F
- Then, I'll move on to
- When I've done that, I'll go on to

G
- I'd then like to conclude with
- Finally, I'll be presenting

簡報的轉折

　　進入「實戰要領」前，先來看看簡報中的「轉折」（making a move）處。進行簡報的過程中，一段資訊進行到另一段資訊間，都須要轉折用語。在簡報的引言中逐步說明每個段落的要點：歡迎句──目的陳述句──預告大綱句。由一個段落進行到下一個時，你就是在 making a move。你得讓觀眾清楚知道轉折在哪裡，他們才跟得上簡報的架構。

　　如果看附錄三 Track 3.1 中第一段簡報的錄音稿，你會看到文字中有「／」這樣的斜線。這些斜線符號標示著段落間的轉折。請仔細看過這些部分後，再繼續讀下去。

Task 3.7

請看 Track 3.1 中第一段簡報的錄音稿。找出所有的斜線符號，從它們出現的位置來看，你注意到什麼？

答案 ┃ 希望你能看出所有的斜線符號都出現在 set-phrase 前面。這表示整個簡報的過程都以 set-phrase 來標示每個段落的轉折。

Task 3.8

Track 3.1

請聽 Track 3.1 的第一段簡報，注意主講者如何運用聲音來標示轉折。

答案 ┃ • 主講者利用音調、還有短暫的停頓，來標示段落之間的轉折。
　　　• 這種標示雖然不明顯，但會影響觀眾對你的信心。
　　　• 不要一個句子接著一個句子、中間沒有停頓地唸下去，這會讓觀眾感到厭煩的。

　　現在來做一些關於「轉折」的練習。

Task 3.9

請看 Track 3.1 中第二及第三段簡報的講稿，用斜線符號標示出轉折。

簡報片段 2

Thanks for coming today. Today, I'm going to be reporting on last year's results. First, I'm going to show you the results for all regions quarter by quarter. Second, I'm going to show you the targets set by the regional office for the year in question, comparing them with the results to give you an idea of our performance. After that, we'll take a look at some of the top performers in each region. When I've done that, I'll go on to compare our performance last year with our main competitors' performance over the same period. I'd then like to conclude with a summary of our market position at the end of last year.

簡報片段 3

Hello everybody, my name is Larry Chen and I represent Better Business Consultancy Incorporated. My presentation today will deal with the problems you are having maintaining your market share. For a start, I'm going to bring you up to speed on the current situation. Then, I plan to discuss the main threats to your market share and to identify those key factors which you can do something about. Third, I'd like to demonstrate how your sister region, Hong Kong, has managed to deal with this issue and to see if there are any lessons we can learn from them. At the end, I'll be suggesting a five-point strategy for dealing with this issue.

答案 ▎ 請翻至書末附錄三「錄音稿」中 Track 3.1 的部分，核對答案。

Task 3.10

Track 3.1

現在用聽的，邊聽邊看上面的講稿。

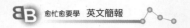
Task 3.11

現在練習大聲朗讀 Track 3.1 中的簡報，並運用聲音來標示轉折。

實戰要領：音調

在這個部分，我們要探討聲音在簡報進行時另外一個非常重要的特點：聲調（intonation）。聲調的抑揚頓挫可說是以聲音譜出的樂曲。英文的語調模式非常簡單：**大體來說，聲調應在句末下降，除非是「yes / no」的問句，這時聲調必須在句子結束時提高。**你也可以利用聲調來強調句中的關鍵字或片語。

以簡報來說，你應該利用聲調來吸引觀眾對簡報的興趣、強調重點、以及表達親切和熱情。在簡報開場的部分尤其重要，你得藉此立刻留下好的印象和影響。先做一個聽力練習，以確保各位了解我的意思。

Task 3.12　　　　　　　　　　　　　　　　 Track 3.3

請聽 Track 3.3。比較各組句子，哪一個句子聽起來比較舒服？哪一個句子的唸法是你在簡報中應該仿效的？為什麼？

答案
- 每一組中第二個句子的唸法是你應該在簡報時使用的。
- 這些句子的聲調範圍較寬，使得主講者的聲音聽起來比較友善、有趣、也較有活力。
- 範圍較廣的聲調有助於留下良好、專業的印象。

好，我們來深入分析這要怎麼做到。請看下面兩個圖解。

圖 1：平常的說話方式

在這個圖中，最上面的線代表你最高的音，底下的線代表你最低的音，中間的線

則是平常的中音。曲線代表大多數人日常會話所使用的聲調範圍。你可以看出曲線維持在中音的附近，高音與低音則不常使用。

圖 2：簡報說話方式

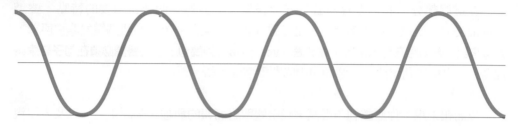

你可以發現這裡的曲線範圍較寬，高、低音也較常使用。這種方式會讓你的聲音更吸引人，也讓觀眾對你的專業能力留下深刻印象。這種聲調模式也廣為專業新聞播報人員和演員所使用。如果我們將這兩條曲線放在一塊，你就可以看出兩者的差異。

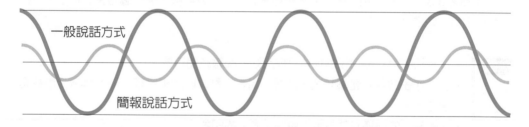

一般說話方式

簡報說話方式

再聽一次 Track 3.3。你應該能聽出第二種說法的聲調都比較寬了吧？聽過幾遍之後，自己試著唸看看。

Task 3.13

練習唸 Track 3.3 中的句子（參考書末附錄三：錄音稿），盡可能把自己的聲調範圍拉到最寬。

答案 ▌ • 或許你會覺得這樣做很蠢！但請記住我在第一章中提到的一個重點：即使你自己覺得很怪，觀眾可不覺得，更重要的是，他們並不曉得你的感覺！
  • 如果你不確定哪裡聲調該提高，哪裡該放低，通常，句中的關鍵字應該要提高

聲調，緊接著就把聲調放低。一般句子的聲調模式為開頭高，結尾低。

- 不過，進行簡報的時候，不應該一直思考這樣的規則，而是應該想著報告的內容與如何讓觀眾了解內容。各位在聽 CD 練習 set-phrases 的發音時，請留意 set-phrases 的聲調。在很自然的狀況下聽和說，而不去想太多，你會表現得更好。

- 還不相信嗎？來做個實驗吧！聽 CNN、 BBC、甚至是當地電視或廣播頻道的新聞。你能否聽出播報人的聲調模式和日常會話大不相同？我們對這種新聞播報方式已經習以為常，而忽略了它與日常會話的差異。這些專業人員都是受過多年的聲音訓練，才能以這種方式播報。這就是為什麼他們聽起來永遠都很吸引人。

- 堅持下去。很快你就不會覺得奇怪了，而且你的簡報會因此而更好。

現在各位對聲調已有比較多的了解，也知道如何運用聲調，請回頭練習本章學過的 set-phrases（簡報必備語庫 3.1），並再聽一遍 Track 3.2 ，用更寬的聲調來練習。

我也強烈建議各位回到第二章，用更寬的聲調練習 set-phrases 。記住，簡報的開場是你在最短的時間達成最大影響力的階段。運用聲調和連音的技巧一定能幫你達到這個目的。

Task 3.14

利用目前學過的 set-phrases 和聲音技巧，請以你自己的簡報題目準備和練習一段簡報的引言。

答案
- 花些時間練習，藉此機會將你在本書前三章中，學到關於簡報引言的用語和技巧整合起來。
- 建議各位把自己的聲音錄下來，然後再聽聽自己努力的成果。
- 要嚴格檢討自己的學習成果。想像自己是台下的觀眾，聽到自己的演講，你喜歡這樣的表現嗎？你覺得這個簡報主講者夠不夠專業？如果答案是否定的，原因是什麼？你得加強的是什麼？
- 練習的時候不要擔心看起來很蠢。練習是很重要的！加油！你一定做得到！

　　本書的第二部分會介紹簡報的「主體」。各位在進入下個章節之前，先回到本章的「學習目標」，檢視一下清單，以確定你沒有漏掉任何一個項目。

PART 2

簡報的主體

UNIT
4
資訊的架構

引言與學習目標

　　第二部分的四個章節是關於簡報的主體。主體是簡報的核心，也是你表達主要理念的地方。主體部分使用的用語大多和內容有關，也就是簡報主題的詞彙。不過，你也需要一些「關節」來安排主體的架構。在進行簡報時，這些關節有助於引導觀眾前進。

　　此章節的重點為：各個簡報段落轉折的 set-phrases ；並建議主體部分應該如何prepare 、 practice 與 perform 。學完本章後，你應該達成的「學習目標」如下：

- ❏ 學會架構主體的 set-phrases 。
- ❏ 了解如何根據「從一般到特定」的模式來架構資訊。
- ❏ 練習聽力和發音。
- ❏ 能以「簡報準備表」practice 和 perform 。

架構資訊的 Set-phrases

　　記得在上個章節中學過的段落轉折技巧嗎？這個技巧在簡報主體部分非常重要。一開始先做些聽力練習。先不要看答案，建議各位至少聽過三遍後，再看答案。

Task 4.1

 Track 4.1

請聽 Track 4.1 的簡報主體部分。算一算你聽到的關節字眼有多少。

答案 ▎這和算的方式有關，不過至少要聽到五、六個。

　　現在接著看標示這些轉折的用語。請做下個 Task。

Task 4.2

請研讀以下的架構 set-phrases。

簡報必備語庫 4.1

• Now, I'd like (you) to V ...	• First / second / third ...
• At this point, I'd like to V ...	• I'm now going to V ...
• I'd like to turn now to n.p. ...	• I'm going to begin by Ving ...
• I want (you) to V ...	• Now, I'm going to V ...
• We need to address two crucial issues: first, ... ; and second, ...	• Let's turn now to n.p. ...
	• Finally, I'm going to V ...
• If I could just move on to n.p. ...	• I'm going to conclude by Ving ...
• There are three main points here: first, ...; second, ...; and third, ...	• I'm going to finish by Ving ...
	• I'd like (you) to V ...
• Right now, we're going to look at n.p. ...	• Let's conclude now by Ving ...
	• That's all I want to say about n.p. ...
• Turning now to n.p. ...	• I'd like to wrap up by Ving ...
• ... beginning with n.p. ...	

★ 📁 語庫小叮嚀

◆ 記得每個 set-phrases 的結尾是 V 、 n.p. 、 n. clause 或 Ving 。

◆ 這些 set-phrases 和第三章中的「標示 set-phrases」類似,這兩者之間的差異在於: 標示 set-phrases 的重點通常放在未來,也就是即將說明的重點;而架構 set-phrases 所引導的重點則在於現在要告訴觀眾的事。

◆ 結語 set-phrases 也可以用在簡報的總結,不過在此是為主體的各個段落做個結束。主 體可能包含好幾個段落,所以在段落轉折時應以這些 set-phrases 說明清楚。

Task 4.3

Track 4.1

再聽一次 Track 4.1 ,並從必備語庫裡勾選你聽到的 set-phrases 。

答案 | 請以書末附錄三的錄音稿核對答案。各位在聽的時候,試著聽聽 set-phrases 和 其他的內容是如何連結的,並注意聲調和速度。

現在各位已學過這些 set-phrases ;接著花些時間練習發音,現在請聽 Track 4.3 。記住,練習的時間愈多,就會愈加流暢,你也會覺得更有自信!

Task 4.4

Track 4.2

請聽 Track 4.2 並同時跟著複誦,練習這些 set-phrases 的發音。

答案 | 至少花 20 分鐘來練習。記住,練習時盡量不要看 set-phrases ,試著專注在聽 力和記憶上。每個 set-phrase 都練習至少五遍之後,再從所有的 set-phrases 中挑出你想加強的,繼續練習直到熟練為止。

請繼續下個 Task 。如同上個章節,建議各位把答案寫在另一張紙上,如此,以 後想要再練習時就可以用不同的 set-phrases 。

Task 4.5

以必備語庫 4.1 的 set-phrases 完成下列簡報。

_____ Ⓐ _____ talk briefly about Asia and three countries in particular, _____ **B** _____ Thailand, which for many years had a strong construction industry. For years the Thailand economy was largely dependent on massive construction projects. Although this industry is still very important, there is now a significant emphasis on tourism and to a certain extent trade of locally produced goods. _____ **C** _____ Korea, which is quite different from Thailand in that it doesn't have such a strong tourism industry, for the simple reason that Korea does not feature strongly as a Western tourist destination. However, Korea has a strong manufacturing base, particularly in heavy industrial goods and consumer electronics. _____ **D** _____ Korea. _____ **E** _____ talk about Malaysia. For many reasons, Malaysia is less typical of other countries in my survey, in that its economic base is far more of an even mix of primary, secondary and tertiary industries. The economy here is more stable, with an equal emphasis on manufacturing, service and tourism. _____ **F** _____ our look at the Asian economies by summarizing the opportunities they present to the company.

答案 建議各位大聲朗讀這段簡報，口頭練習的方式會比寫答案卷有用得多。因為簡報需要的是口語的技巧，而非書寫技巧。
注意 set-phrase 的結尾，以及 set-phrase 是如何連接句子的其他部分。如果有錄音機，可以把自己的練習錄下來，聽聽看有哪裡需要改進。
接著請核對答案。

A
• Now, I'd like to
• At this point, I'd like to
• I want to
• I'm now going to
• Now I'm going to
• I'd like to

B
• beginning with

tertiary〔ˋtɝʃɪˏɛrɪ〕*adj.* 第三的

C
- I'd like to turn now to
- If I could just move on to
- Right now, we are going to look at
- Turning now to
- Let's turn now to

D
- That's all I want to say about

E
- Now, I'd like to
- At this point, I'd like to
- I want to
- I'm now going to
- Now I'm going to
- I'd like to

F
- Finally I'm going to wrap up
- I'm going to conclude
- I'm going to finish

　　現在各位應能了解如何運用這些 set-phrases 來架構主體的資訊；接著像上一個章節一樣練習「轉折」的部分。

Task 4.6

在 Task 4.5 的簡報片段中，請在主講者轉折的地方畫上斜線。看得出轉折屬於何種類嗎？

答案	
... three countries in particular, / beginning with ...	這個轉折是從一般資訊（亞洲）轉到亞洲三國的第一個例子（泰國）。
... locally produced goods. / I'd like to turn now to ...	第一個例子（泰國）和第二個例子（韓國）之間的轉折。

| ... Korea. / Now, I'd like to ... | 從第二個例子（韓國）到第三個例子（馬來西亞）之間的轉折。 |
| ... services and tourism. / Finally, I'm going to ... | 從第三個例子轉折到主體的下一個要點，說明該公司在各個國家的機會的一般敘述。 |

各位應該能很清楚地看出這種「從一般到特定」的結構：一般敘述（亞洲三國）；特定敘述（泰國、韓國、馬來西亞）；下個一般敘述。這種「從一般到特定」的結構是組織英文資訊最常見的方法。各位應該也可看出如何利用 set-phrases 來標示這些轉折，請以書末的錄音稿核對答案。

再來練習使用這些 set-phrases，不過這次換個主題，做完後，再聽 CD 核對答案。

Task 4.7 Track 4.3

請以必備語庫 4.1 的 set-phrases 完成下列簡報，然後邊聽 Track 4.3，邊核對答案。

_____Ⓐ_____ look in a bit more detail at the results of the survey for each segment of the market. _____Ⓑ_____ looking at the youth segment. _____Ⓒ_____, most respondents said the product line was relevant to their lifestyle, _____Ⓓ_____, a significant number said they wanted to own the complete line; and _____Ⓔ_____, a smaller number said they only wanted one product from the line and had no intention of buying more. _____Ⓕ_____ the main-wage-earner segment, a much smaller number of respondents said they were interested in the product line, and most of these were female. Most of the people in this segment did not express much interest in the product. _____Ⓖ_____ the senior citizen segment. We had a fantastic response here, especially among women. All the respondents said they would like to own more of the product line, but were not happy with the packaging, saying it was hard to open. _____Ⓗ_____ summarizing the key recommendations from the market survey.

答案 同上一個 Task ，各位需要注意 set-phrase 的結尾。我相信各位現在對此應該都很在行了，對不對？！接著核對答案吧。

A • Now, I'd like to
• At this point, I'd like to
• I want to
• I'm now going to
• Now I'm going to
• I'd like to

B • I'm going to begin by

C • There are three main points here: first
• We need to address three crucial issues: first,

D • second,

E • third,

F • Now, I'd like to look at
• At this point, I'd like to look at
• I want to look at
• I'm now going to look at
• Now I'm going to look at

G • I'd like to turn now to
• If I could just move on to
• Right now, we're going to look at
• Turning now to
• Let's turn now to

H • Let's conclude now by
• I'm going to conclude by
• I'm going to finish by
• I'd like to wrap up by

再練習標示出轉折處，看看這段簡報的「從一般到特定」的結構。

Task 4.8

將 Task 4.7 簡報片段的轉折處以斜線標示出來，看看主講者做了哪種轉折？

答案 │ 希望這次各位能更輕易地看出這種「從一般到特定」的結構，並看出 set-phrases 如何標示出這些轉折。以 set-phrases 標示轉折對於吸引觀眾的注意是很重要的。如果觀眾能掌握簡報的架構，自然比較容易吸收你的想法。

... each segment of the market. / I'm going to ...	這是從一般資訊（各市場區隔的意見調查結果）轉折到第一個例子（年輕人的市場）
... the youth segment. / There are three ...	這個轉折讓聽眾知道現在正在談論第一個例子（年輕人的市場），進而將年輕人的市場分為三個特定的例子：「大多數的受訪者」、「很多」和「少數」。每個轉折都以「首先」、「第二」、和「第三」的 set-phrases 來標示。
... no intention of buying more. / Now, I'd like to ...	從第一個例子（年輕人的市場）轉折到第二個例子（主要受薪族群）。
... interest in the product. / I'd like to ...	從第二個例子轉折到第三個例子（銀髮族）。
... hard to open. / Let's conclude ...	從第三個例子轉折到下個段落的一般說明（主要建議摘要）。

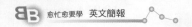

實戰要領：簡報準備表

　　誠如我在本書「前言」中所提及，做英文簡報和以自己的母語做簡報很不一樣。因為語言上的問題，很容易讓觀眾覺得無聊。在此，我要探討各位在 prepare、practice 和 perform 英文簡報可能碰到的問題、以及如何克服這些問題，以解決語言對簡報造成的障礙。在做下個 Task 之前，請花幾分鐘的時間想想自己 prepare、practice 和 perform 的方式，你在各個階段採用了哪些步驟或程序。

Task 4.9

請看下列清單，勾選和你採用的方式最接近的選項。

（　　）**1.** 我把簡報內容逐字寫下來，就像一篇文章一樣，然後大聲朗誦。

（　　）**2.** 我把簡報內容逐字寫下來，就像一篇文章一樣，然後背下來。

（　　）**3.** 我寫好幾頁的筆記，然後逐一唸出來。

（　　）**4.** 我寫好幾頁的筆記，然後試著背下來。

（　　）**5.** 我在卡片上寫下標題，並在我的簡報中提到這些標題。

（　　）**6.** 我不寫任何筆記、或寫下任何東西；我只準備 PowerPoint 的投影片。

答案 不管你選擇的是哪個選項，都不是進行英文簡報的有效方式。讓我們逐項來檢討：

1. 記住簡報是一種活動。光是照本宣科並不是有效的溝通方式。你得和觀眾有眼神上的接觸，如果只是看著講稿一直唸，還不如把講稿發給觀眾，把簡報取消算了！

2. 我敢保證你一定會忘詞！當你絞盡腦汁想要恢復記憶時，觀眾可不好受。這絕對不是個好主意。

3. 寫筆記固然不錯，可是用哪種筆記？有多少用處？這裡也會有第一項照本宣科的問題。

4. 背誦絕對是簡報的墳墓。

5. 卡片是個好主意，可是萬一這些卡片掉了一地，撿起來後順序全部都亂了，怎麼辦？那可不妙！

6. 如果你的電腦故障呢？還是 PowerPoint 程式有病毒呢？

這些「prepare—practice—perform」的方式都遺漏了 practice 的階段。 Practice 是成功簡報的關鍵。

讓我們看看從 prepare 、 practice 順利進行到 perform 的方法。下列的「簡報準備表」可以應用在 prepare 、 practice 和 perform 各階段。各位可利用這份表單來準備和組織資訊、選擇用語，並加以練習；在實際做簡報時，可以這份表單作為記憶的輔助工具。

簡報準備表

標　　題	在此填上簡報的標題、日期、觀眾和目的	
日　　期		
觀　　眾		
目　　的		
你想要使用的 **set-phrases**		關鍵內容的 **word partnerships**
在此寫下要用來標示轉折、和說明簡報階段的 set-phrases		在此以 word partnerships 寫下關鍵的內容資訊

接著看看完成後的表格，就能了解如何運用這份準備表。請做以下的 Task 。

Task 4.10

看看下列的簡報準備表，然後和 Task 4.5 的簡報片段、或 Track 4.1 的錄音稿做比較。
注意主講者的準備方式，關鍵內容的 word partnerships 記在右邊，然後在左邊寫下一些
架構的 set-phrases 。

簡報準備表

題 目	Expanding into Asia
日 期	Today
觀 眾	Department heads
目 的	To persuade the company to open a branch in Malaysia

你想要使用的 set-phrases	關鍵內容的 word partnerships
Now I'd like to talk briefly about ...	Three countries in Asia
beginning with ...	**Thailand — before**
	• strong construction industry
	• economy dependent on massive construction projects
	Thailand — now
	• significant emphasis on tourism
	• trade of locally produced goods
Let's turn now to ...	**Korea**
	• no strong tourist industry: not a Western tourist destination
	• strong manufacturing base: heavy industrial goods / consumer electronics
That's all I want to say about Korea.	
I'm now going to talk about ...	**Malaysia**

	• economic base: primary / secondary / tertiary industries
	• stable economy
	• equal emphasis on manufacturing, service and tourism
Finally, I'm going to conclude by summarizing ...	• opportunities they present to us

答案 這樣的準備方式能讓你專注在簡報用語上。在 prepare 時，你可以從本書的必備語庫選擇要用的 set-phrases，並找出架構資訊的 set-phrases 和關鍵內容的 word partnerships；在 practice 和 perform 時，只須從左到右地看下去，如以下圖示。如此，你只須瞄一眼就知道簡報進行到哪，也能持續維持和觀眾的眼神接觸。各位得練習幾次才能熟練。

簡報準備表

題　目	Expanding into Asia
日　期	Today
觀　眾	Department heads
目　的	To persuade the company to open a branch in Malaysia

你想要使用的 set-phrases	關鍵內容的 word partnerships
Now I'd like to talk briefly about ...	Three countries in Asia
beginning with ...	**Thailand — before**
	• strong construction industry
	• economy dependent on massive construction projects
	Thailand — now
	• significant emphasis on tourism
	• trade of locally produced goods
Let's turn now to ...	**Korea**

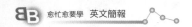
	• no strong tourist industry: not a Western tourist destination
	• strong manufacturing base: heavy industrial goods / consumer electronics
That's all I want to say about Korea.	
I'm now going to talk about ...	**Malaysia**
	• economic base: primary / secondary / tertiary industries
	• stable economy
	• equal emphasis on manufacturing, service and tourism
Finally, I'm going to conclude by summarizing...	• opportunities they present to us

Task 4.11

Track 4.1

再聽一次 Track 4.1 ，邊聽邊看著 Task 4.10 中的簡報準備表。

　　抓到訣竅了嗎？聽過幾遍之後就會明白我的意思。接著，體驗一下如何使用這準備表吧，請做以下的 Task 。

Task 4.12

現在以 Task 4.10 中準備表的內容來練習做場簡報吧。

Task 4.13

請以 Task 4.7 關於市場研究調查的簡報片段，填寫這份「簡報準備表」。見範例。

簡報準備表

題　目	Repositioning our brand
日　期	Tomorrow
觀　眾	Department Heads
目　的	To get budget and approval for a new marketing campaign aimed at main wage earning segment

你想要使用的 set-phrases	關鍵內容的 word partnerships
Turning now to ...	main-wage-earner segment

答案 在 word partnerships 欄位裡使用的字可能會略有不同；但在 set-phrases 欄位，答案則應該一樣。接著請以下頁的表格核對答案。

你想要使用的 set-phrases	關鍵內容的 word partnerships
I'm now going to ...	survey results each market segment
I'm going to begin by...	youth segment

There are three main points here:	**First:** product line relevant to lifestyle
	Second: significant number own
	           complete line
	Third: smaller number only wanted one
	           product, no intention of buying
	           more

Turning now to ...	**main-wage-earner segment**
	• smaller number interested in the
	  product line
	• mostly female
	• most people not much interest in
	  product

Let's turn now to...	**senior citizen segment**
	• fantastic response, especially
	  amongst women
	• all the respondents like to own more
	  of the product line
	• **BUT** not happy with the packaging:
	  hard to open

I'd like to wrap up by summarizing ...	key recommendations

　　接著利用以上的準備表來練習做簡報吧。記住，練習時要留意在第二、三章節中學過的發音。練習幾次直到你能熟練地運用這份表單。當你覺得有信心時，就可以做下一個 Task 。

Task 4.14

以自己曾做過的簡報內容來完成「簡報準備表」，並練習如何在簡報中使用。

這個 Task 為本章畫下句點。請回到本章的「學習目標」，看看你達成了多少。

UNIT 5

說明資訊：
準備視覺材料

引言與學習目標

在上個章節中，我們探討過如何架構資訊。在接下來的兩個章節，我們將進而探討如何說明資訊，特別是透過視覺材料。我所說的視覺材料，指的是簡報中使用的投影片。這個章節的重點在於準備視覺材料，下一章則在探討視覺材料的使用。

在運用視覺材料時可能會犯一些錯誤。請看以下幾點，你是否犯了其中的錯誤呢？

- 投影片太多。
- 投影片包含太多資訊。
- 投影片讓觀眾覺得困惑。
- 投影片包含了非必要的資訊。
- 在準備、練習、進行簡報時，過度強調投影片。

這個章節會告訴各位如何準備輔助簡報的視覺材料。這個章節沒有語言練習的部分，但這裡介紹的重點攸關著簡報的成功，所以各位應該熟讀此章，務求充分掌握其中要點。

本章節結束時，你應該能夠：

☐ 對於觀眾如何吸收資訊有更清楚的了解。
☐ 能運用這方面的知識設計更好的視覺材料。
☐ 了解高、低密度資訊的差異。
☐ 改善 prepare 、 practice 和 perform 的程序。
☐ 練習聽力，增加對這些重點的了解。

成功簡報的要素

一開始，請各位想想自己見過最棒和最糟糕的簡報，並列舉出原因。之後再做下一個 Task，看看簡報成功的要素為何。

Task 5.1

將下列簡報的要素依重要性排序，你覺得哪一個要素對於簡報的成功最為重要？

( ) The audience
( ) The content
( ) The equipment
( ) The handouts
( ) The presenter's voice, delivery, and presence
( ) The Q&A session
( ) The refreshments
( ) The room
( ) The visuals

答案 下列 1、2、3 的重要性順序是固定的。其他要素的排序依據各人的經驗，不見得會認同我的排法。不過前三項對簡報成功最重要的要素，希望各位和我的看法一致。

1. The presenter's voice, delivery, and presence
   簡報者的聲音、陳述方式、儀表
   務必記住，簡報成功的關鍵是「你」！你的聲音、你的表情、你的肢體語言和簡報的專業性。➡ 你攸關著簡報的成敗。

2. The content 內容

| Word List |

refreshment〔rɪˋfrɛʃmənt〕 *n.* 茶點；便餐

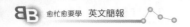

身為主講者,你得有東西可以介紹,也就是你的內容。視覺材料並不是所有的內容。➡ 內容應該讓觀眾覺得有意思,而且和他們相關,並能幫助你達成簡報的目的。

3. The audience 觀眾

簡報是一種活動,觀眾關係著簡報的成功與否。他們提出的問題、他們在簡報後的談論所帶來的效益、以及你和他們建立的關係:這些對於簡報的成功都有著關鍵性的影響。➡ 你應該專注在和觀眾的溝通上。

The Visuals 視覺材料

視覺材料的目的是支援、說明或解釋內容。稍後會進一步說明其中細節。➡ 視覺材料應該易看、易讀、而且易理解。

The Handouts 講義

講義提供的是輔助性的資料、更詳盡的圖表,可以藉此作為提醒重點的工具。不要在簡報一開始就發放講義,這樣會使觀眾分心。➡ 講義不一定得和投影片一樣。

The Equipment 設備

確定設備能順利運作是簡報者的責任。在觀眾進場前先架設好投影機、螢幕和筆記型電腦。一定要知道簡報室裡的燈光如何開關。如果須使用麥克風,也須清楚怎麼開關、以及如何避免回音。把簡報存放在 CD ROM 或軟碟裡是個好主意,萬一筆記型電腦當機,你還是能使用另外一台電腦來繼續簡報。➡ 專業的簡報者總是得想好設備失靈的應變方案。

The Q&A session 問答部分

問答的部分難以預測,所以無法練習。許多簡報者對此都相當畏懼,但是無須擔心。只要你很熟悉簡報的資料,就應該沒有問題。在第九章中會進一步說明如何處理問答的部分。➡ 問答這個部分是達成目的、以及和觀眾溝通的最後機會。

The Room 簡報室

簡報室的規模、和裡頭的座椅設備會決定你的簡報風格。如果簡報室很大、有很多的聽眾,那你會需要麥克風,說話要慢點,動作得大些。如果簡報室的規模小,那

就不須麥克風，可以比較親切的語調，加強眼神的接觸。 ➡ 優秀的簡報者會在觀眾進場前先瞭解簡報室的狀況。

The Refreshments 茶點

希望各位沒有把這放在第一位！

準備視覺材料

視覺材料可以分爲兩種：「架構視覺材料」和「內容視覺材料」。

架構視覺材料

是在進行簡報時，用來顯示簡報架構的視覺材料。包括了標題及大綱的投影片。這些視覺資料標明簡報的各個段落，就如同一本書中章節的標題。這些投影片不應該納入講義之內。

內容視覺材料

是在呈現數據、說明和比較圖表時使用的投影片。這些應該納入講義之內。

Task 5.2

看看下列的投影片，判斷它們屬於架構、還是內容投影片。

1.

Marketing strategy 2004

2.
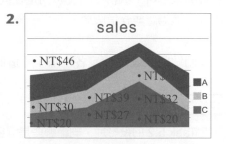

3.

achieving success

4.

答案　• 1 和 3 屬於架構投影片，2 和 4 屬於內容投影片。
　　　• 1 和 3 投影片就像是書中的章節標題，2 和 4 投影片則是關於你的目的、以及觀眾應該知道的事情。

　　希望各位能清楚看出這兩種投影片之間的差異。現在讓我們更深入地探討投影片中的資訊應該如何呈現。

　　在選擇呈現資訊最適合的方式時，得問問自己這兩個問題：

1. 觀眾如何接收資訊？

　　大腦接收資訊主要是透過兩個管道：眼睛（visual channel 「視覺管道」）和耳朵（audio channel「聽覺管道」）；也就是說，你可以「讀」電子郵件裡的資訊，或「聽」簡報。大多數的證據顯示，讀和聽兩件事同時進行時，會降低大腦記住資訊的能力。這表示當觀眾分心讀投影片時，他們吸收你正在表達的資訊的能力會降低，這會令你難以達成簡報的目的。

2. 資訊屬於哪種類型？

　　不過你可考慮想要呈現的資訊類型，然後將 audio 和 visual channels 結合以強化訊息的力量。資訊有兩種：高密度（high density）和低密度（low density）的資訊。高密度指的是許多文字和圖表在極小的空間裡呈現，這讓 audio 和 visual channels 需要更多時間來解析；低密度的資訊則是在同樣的空間裡呈現較少的資訊。低密度的資訊比較容易透過這些管道吸收。

　　讓我們做些 Task，確定各位都了解這個重點。

Task 5.3

再看一次 Task 5.2 的投影片，判斷哪些是低密度、哪些是高密度的資訊。

答案　架構投影片（1 和 3）是屬於低密度資訊：上頭只有一、兩個字，所以很快就可以被讀取。第四張內容投影片是屬於低密度資訊，第二張則是高密度資訊，上頭包括太多資訊，觀眾須花些時間來讀。然而，他們在讀的時候，就不會聽你講話。

Task 5.4 Track 5.1

聽 Track 5.1 中的兩段簡報。哪一段屬於高密度資訊，哪一段屬於低密度資訊？

答案
- 第一段顯然是屬於高密度的資訊，包含了許多圖表和資料。用讀的會比較容易吸收、記住這些資訊。
- 第二段是屬於低密度資訊。很容易就可以掌握重點。

Task 5.5

現在把 Track 5.1 中的兩段簡報和以下的圖配對。

1.

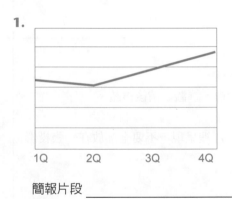

簡報片段 ＿＿＿＿＿＿＿＿＿＿＿＿＿

2.

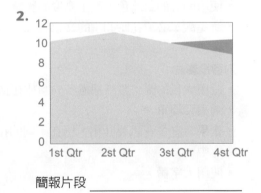

簡報片段 ＿＿＿＿＿＿＿＿＿＿＿＿＿

答案
- **1.** 簡報片段 ＿＿1＿＿ **2.** 簡報片段 ＿＿2＿＿
- 各位可能覺得光是用聽的，很難將簡報片段 1 和投影片 1 連在一塊。這並不讓人驚訝，因為高密度的資訊很難透過 audio channel 吸收。翻至書末看看錄音稿，你會發現用讀的就很容易吸收。

請看以下的表格，彙整了到目前為止的重點。

	低密度資訊	高密度資訊
視覺管道：讀	容易吸收	容易吸收，但速度慢。
聽覺管道：聽	容易吸收	難以吸收

各位應該時時謹記在心的是：觀眾在讀視覺資料時，他們就不會聽你說話。如果觀眾不聽你說話，簡報的目的就難以達成。所以，設計觀眾無須花時間讀、只要一看就可以理解的投影片，才能讓他們專心在你的報告。你才是成功的關鍵，不是你的投影片！

下列重點是在準備視覺資料時的重要準則。

設計投影片的技巧：

架構投影片
- 只須一、兩個字即可。
- 使用大的字體：填滿螢幕。
- 使用明亮的對比色，產生高度的影響力。
- 避免觀眾必須花時間讀的文字。

內容投影片
- 避免大量的圖：應該把過多的圖放在講義裡，讓觀眾稍後再讀。
- 圖表要簡單。
- 如果有許多資訊要介紹，應在不同的投影片裡呈現，不要全部放在一張投影片中。
- 使用大字體。

最重要的原則是：**不要設計觀眾必須花時間讀的投影片。**

各位不妨回頭看看第三章中的投影片，那些投影片符合這些標準嗎？

實戰要領：架構資訊的技巧

　　各位到目前爲止所學到的重點，可能有許多和你們過去設計投影片的方式不同，所以不太確定我的說法是否正確。接下來我要進一步探討架構資訊的實用技巧。希望這些實用的技巧能協助各位準備更有效的英文簡報。現在請做以下的 Task 。

Task 5.6

請看下列的項目，勾選出和你 prepare 、 practice 和 perform 簡報的方式最接近的選項。做練習的時候，想想自己實際準備簡報的經驗。

準備 PREPARATION

(　　) **1.** I start my preparation by designing slides.

(　　) **2.** I structure my presentation around my slides.

(　　) **3.** I put as much information as possible on each slide.

(　　) **4.** I print the slides and give them out as handouts.

(　　) **5.** I use roughly 80 to 100 slides in a presentation.

練習 PRACTICE

(　　) **6.** I practice by reading through my notes until I know them.

表現 PERFORMANCE

(　　) **7.** I present every piece of information on every slide.

(　　) **8.** My presentations last roughly three hours.

(　　) **9.** I hope my audience is focusing on the slides and what they are telling them.

答案 　請看下列這些敘述，你都認同嗎？

1. I start my preparation by designing slides.

我從設計投影片開始準備簡報。

通常大家都是這樣開始準備的。一得知要做簡報，就會打開電腦開始設計投影片。

2. I structure my presentation around my slides.

我一邊準備投影片、一邊架構我的簡報。

有些人在準備之初沒有思考結構的問題，而是在設計投影片的過程中逐漸找出結構。也可能是依據蒐集到的資訊、圖表或數據的順序來決定結構。

3. I put as much information as possible on each slide.

我在每張投影片中都盡可能地塞入資訊。

許多人以為資訊愈多愈好。其實不見得是對的。如果給予觀眾的資訊太多，可能會有 information overload（資訊過載）的風險。

4. I print the slides and give them out as handouts.

我將投影片印出當作講義發給大家。

這是製作講義迅速、簡單的方法。然而，這樣的講義會有效嗎？

5. I use roughly 80 to 100 slides in a presentation.

我在一場簡報裡使用大約 80 到 100 張的投影片。

有些公司會提供員工製作簡報的範本，這些範本可能會非常長，然而，你不須使用範本裡全部的投影片！有些人用了很多投影片是因為希望觀眾會專注在投影片、而不是他們身上。他們對自己的簡報能力缺乏自信，你們也是這樣嗎？

6. I practice by reading through my notes until I know them.

我會照著自己的筆記唸，一直到懂了為止。

如果你是以母語進行簡報，可以用這種方式練習。

7. I present every piece of information on every slide.

我在投影片上呈現所有的資訊。

有多少資訊就呈現多少，對不對？那資訊過載怎麼辦？

8. My presentations last roughly three hours.

我的簡報持續大約三個小時。

或四個小時。或五個小時。（打哈欠……）

9. I hope my audience is focusing on the slides and what they are telling them.

我希望觀眾專注在投影片和其中的內容。

我的投影片是花了好幾個小時準備的，真的很重要！而且，如果觀眾專注在投影片上，就不會盯著我，我也就不會覺得緊張。

以上這些程序和解說，對於英文簡報而言都是不正確的。

接著我們來看看一些 prepare 、 practice 和 perform 英文簡報程序的其他選擇。

Task 5.7

以下是針對 Task 5.6 錯誤述敘的訂正。請將以下的選項和 Task 5.6 的選項配對，在括弧內填入適當號碼，見範例。

準備 PREPARATION

(*9*) I hope my audience is focusing on me and what I'm telling them.

(   ) I only put key information on my slides.

(   ) I practice by reading aloud and working on my pronunciation.

(   ) I start my preparation by knowing how my purpose can best be supported by slides.

(   ) I structure my presentation around my purpose.

練習 PRACTICE

(   ) I summarize the key points of the slide in accordance with my purpose.

表演 PERFORMANCE

(   ) I use a maximum of 20 slides in a presentation.

(   ) My presentations are designed to last no longer than 50 minutes.

(   ) The slides I show are simplified versions of my handouts.

答案

(*9*) I hope my audience is focusing on me and what I'm telling them.

我希望觀眾專注在我身上和我要告訴他們的內容。

記得我先前所說的嗎？ ➡ 你才是成功的關鍵，不是你的投影片

(*3*) I only put key information on the slide.

我只放關鍵資訊在投影片上。

注意，投影片上的資訊密度須低，只放絕對必要的資訊在上頭。其他比較細節的圖表、數據等可以包含在講義裡發給觀眾。簡報的時候可以提及講義，不過建議在簡報結束時才發講義，如此，進行簡報時觀眾才會專心，不會分心在講義上。

(6) I practice by reading aloud and working on my pronunciation.

我練習時會大聲唸，並注意我的發音。

準備英文簡報時，須花時間來練習發音，並事先演練簡報，而不只是一直默唸講稿。可以利用第四章中的「簡報準備表」，找個安靜的地方或在鏡子前面練習。你可能覺得這樣練習有點蠢，不過這是有效的練習方式！多花心思在引言和總結的部分，因為這二部分的影響力最大。

(1) I start my preparation by knowing how my purpose can best be supported by slides.

準備簡報的一開始，先思考如何以投影片來協助自己達成目的。

一開始都須先清楚設定簡報的目的。一旦目的設定完成，其他的事項（簡報該包含哪些內容、該如何架構）也就容易決定。

(2) I structure my presentation around my purpose.

我根據我的目的來架構簡報。

想想簡報的目的，絕對有助你判斷簡報該包含什麼內容、刪掉什麼資訊，以及如何架構內容。

(7) I summarize the key points of the slide in accordance with my purpose.

我根據我的目的，將重點摘要在投影片上。

如果你逐一說明投影片上所有的資訊，可能會讓觀眾覺得無趣。記住，投影片和你的解說，應該配合你的目的。簡短、而且要切中要點。

(5) I use a maximum of 20 slides in a presentation.

我簡報裡最多使用 20 張投影片。

這個數字並不是規定，而是建議。然而，投影片並不是簡報的主角，你才是。如果投影片數目超過 20-25 張，簡報就會過於冗長，觀眾會覺得無趣。如果投影片太多，就得重新考慮簡報該包含哪些資訊、或將簡報分為兩場、或是在講義裡放入較多的資訊。

(8) My presentations are designed to last no longer than 50 minutes.

我的簡報預計不會超過 50 分鐘。

有關注意力持續時間的研究顯示，大多數人的注意力無法超過 50 分鐘至 1 個小時。將簡報維持在 50 分鐘之內，其餘時間進行問答。如果簡報必須進行得比較久，那就在 50 分鐘後休息，讓觀眾有時間伸展筋骨、上廁所、問問題等。你會發現，觀眾在休息後的反應比較好，你達成目的的機會也比較高。

（ *4* ）The slides I show are simplified versions of my handouts.
我顯示的投影片是講義的簡化版。
不要把投影片直接列印出來當作講義。投影片裡許多資訊是不須觀眾去讀的，
諸如大多數的架構投影片。把講義當作達成目的的輔助性資料。

　　好了，這個章節包含了較多的理論。然而，希望你覺得實用，而且能理解我說的
重點。在本章結束之前，各位不妨回頭看看本章的「學習目標」，你達成了多少？幾
天後再回來複習本章節，確定自己掌握了其中的要點。此外，當在聽別人的簡報時，
也可以本章的要點和程序來審視他們的簡報。

UNIT / 6

視覺材料的運用

引言與學習目標

上一章學過了如何準備有效的視覺材料。這個章節要來看看如何有效地運用這些視覺材料。最常見的錯誤就是將視覺材料中的資料一五一十地報告出來。哪些資料有必要向觀眾解說是須經過挑選的。

本章節將介紹使用視覺材料的四個程序、及其相關的用語。研讀完本章，你應該達到的學習目標如下：

☐ 學會說明視覺材料的四個程序，並能運用自如。
☐ 學會這四個程序的相關 set-phrases。
☐ 了解如何利用視覺材料的技巧。
☐ 訓練聽力。

使用視覺材料的四個程序

Task 6.1

Track 6.1 & 6.2

請聽 Track 6.1 與 6.2 ，看看簡報主講者如何呈現視覺材料。

1. 每位簡報者的視覺材料各為什麼主題？
2. 在每個 track 中你聽到了幾個轉折？
3. 主講者如何維持觀眾的興趣？

答案

1. Track 6.1 的主題為銷售數字。 Track 6.2 則是護膚產品的市場區隔。

2. 每個 track 中都有四個轉折。你的答案多或少於四都沒關係，稍後再回頭討論這點。

3. 各位是否注意到主講者如何運用停頓、音調、及流暢的速度？是否注意到主講者花在每個視覺材料上的時間都很短？這些都有助於維持觀眾的興趣。

現在來看看引言中提及的四個程序：

使用視覺材料的四個程序

1. **介紹投影片的主題**。這一點非常重要，必須讓觀眾對投影片的內容先有個概念，再深入探討細節。

2. **強調相關資料**。把觀眾的注意力帶到有助於達成目的的投影片上。不必把每個數字、每行字、月份都提出來加以說明。只要挑出和目的密切相關的資料加以說明即可。和目的沒有太直接關係的資料可不予理會。

3. **摘要說明關鍵要點**。只是挑出相關資料來說明稍嫌不足，還得告知觀眾這些資料的重要性在哪，以及由這些資料可以得出什麼結論。你必須解說、利用這些資料以達到簡報的目的。

4. **進行下一張投影片**。關鍵的資料都提出和解釋過，就可以進行到下一張投影片。此時請再從第一個程序重新開始。

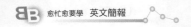

因此，總結來說，四個程序如下：

1. 介紹投影片的主題。
2. 強調相關資料。
3. 摘要說明關鍵要點。
4. 進行下一張投影片。

Task 6.2　　　　　　　　　　　　　　　Track 6.3 & 6.4

請聽 Track 6.3 和 6.4，看看主講者如何運用視覺材料。

1. 主講者的投影片各為什麼主題？
2. 主講者如何利用上述四個程序解說這些主題。
3. 主講者在進行每一個程序時，使用了哪些 set-phrases？將這些 set-phrases 寫下來。

答案　**1.** Track 6.3 的主題是：過去三年的銷售數字與同期目標數字的比較結果。
　　　　Track 6.4 則為：三個主要產品線在三個不同市場的成本與利潤。
　　　2. 如果無法抓出要領，回頭將四個程序再看一次，然後再聽一遍。
　　　3. 如果沒有聽出所有的 set-phrases 不用擔心。稍後會再練習這些 set-phrases。
　　　也可以用 Track 6.1 和 Track 6.2 來做這個練習，加強聽力。

接著來看看在串聯這四個程序的過程中會使用到的 set-phrases。請做 Task 6.3。

Task 6.3

將下列這些用語分類，並填入下表。

1. As you can see, ...
2. Going on to n.p. ...
3. I'd like to draw your attention to n.p. ...
4. I'd like to draw your attention to the fact that + n. clause
5. I'd now like you to look at n.p. ...

6. If you look at this (chart/graph/table), you can see n.p. ...

7. If you look at this (chart/graph/table), you can see that + n. clause

8. If you look here you can see n.p. ...

9. If you look here you can see that + n. clause

10. It is clear from this (chart/graph/table/movement) that + n. clause

11. It is clear from the general movement that + n. clause

12. Let me draw your attention to n.p. ...

13. Let me elaborate on n.p. ...

14. Let me expand on n.p. ...

15. Let's turn now to n.p. (,which we can see here.)

16. Look at the n.p. ...

17. Look at the way that + n. clause

18. Moving on to the next slide, ...

19. Notice how + n. clause

20. Notice the n.p. ...

21. On this slide we've got n.p. ...

22. These figures suggest that + n. clause

23. These statistics show n.p. ...

24. These statistics show that + n. clause

25. This graph displays n.p. ...

26. This next (chart/graph/table) shows us that + n. clause

27. This next slide gives us the figures for n.p. ...

28. This slide describes n.p. ...

29. This slide shows n.p. ...

30. This slide shows that + n. clause

31. We can see from this graph that + n. clause

32. Notice that + n. clause

| Word List |

elaborate [ɪˈlæbərɪt] *v.* 詳述

介紹投影片的主題 Introduce the Topic

強調相關資料 Highlight Relevant Information

摘要說明關鍵要點 Summarize with the Key Point

進行下一張投影片 Move to the Next Slide

答案 ┃ 請以必備語庫 6.1 核對答案。

簡報必備語庫 6.1

介紹投影片的主題 Introduce the Topic

- I'd now like you to look at n.p. ...
- If you look at this (chart/graph/table), you can see n.p. ...
- If you look at this (chart/graph/table), you can see that + n. clause
- If you look here you can see n.p. ...
- If you look here you can see that + n. clause
- On this slide we've got n.p. ...
- These statistics show n.p. ...

- This graph displays n.p. ...
- This next (chart/graph/table) shows us that + n. clause
- This next slide gives us the figures for n.p. ...
- This slide describes n.p. ...
- This slide shows n.p. ...

強調相關資料 Highlight Relevant Information

- As you can see, ...
- I'd like to draw your attention to n.p. ...
- I'd like to draw your attention to the fact that + n. clause
- I'd now like you to look at n.p. ...
- Let me draw your attention to n.p. ...
- Look at the n.p. ...
- Look at the way that + n. clause
- Notice how + n. clause
- Notice that + n. clause
- Notice the n.p. ...
- We can see from this graph that + n. clause

摘要說明關鍵要點 Summarize with the Key Point

- It is clear from this (chart/graph/table/movement) that + n. clause
- It is clear from the general movement that + n. clause
- Let me elaborate on n.p. ...
- Let me expand on n.p. ...
- These figures suggest that + n. clause
- These statistics show that + n. clause
- This slide shows that + n. clause

進行下一張投影片 Move to the Next Slide

- Going on to n.p. ...
- Let's turn now to n.p. (,which we can see here.)
- Moving on to the next slide, ...

以上的分類，也許會出現一些重疊。例如： These statistics show ... 就很難決定該分類到「介紹投影片的主題」或「摘要說明關鍵要點」，在這兩個程序中你都有可能用到這個 set-phrase。另，在介紹一連串的投影片時，「進行下一張投影片」和「介紹投影片的主題」的時間間隔極短，二者並無明顯的界線。這部分的重點是熟悉這些 set-phrases，並能以清晰的發音說出來，如此，觀眾對你主講簡報的角色就不會失去信心。

Task 6.4 Track 6.5

請聽 Track 6.5 練習 set-phrases 的發音。

> 答案 花二十分鐘練習。記住，練習時不要看 set-phrases，專注在聽力和記憶力。每個 set-phrase 聽至少五遍，然後再看一遍必備語庫，挑出你想加強的部分，練習到熟練為止。

Task 6.5  Track 6.1 – 6.4

再聽一遍 Track 6.1 到 6.4。一邊聽一邊將主講者所使用的 set-phrases 勾選出來。

> 答案 請翻至書末附錄的錄音稿來核對答案。留意 CD 中主講者如何將 set-phrases 和其他內容串聯在一起，以及主講者的音調和速度。

接著，練習使用 set-phrases 來講解視覺材料。請做下一個 Task。答案不一定得和 CD 的內容相同，不過必須確定你填入的 set-phrases 用法無誤。

Task 6.6

由必備語庫 6.1 的 set-phrases 中，選出適當者填到空格上。

簡報片段 1

OK. _____ Ⓐ _____ the sales figures for the last quarter of this year compared with the figures for the last quarter of last year. _____ Ⓑ _____ this year's figures are much lower than the previous year's. Let me remind you, however, these figures are not quite complete.

This is because we are still waiting for the results from a sales person who has been on leave. In general, _____ **C** _____ results this year are going to be comparable to the results from last year. _____ **D** _____ costs, _____ **D** _____ .

簡報片段 2

_____ **A** _____ this pie chart, which shows the market segmentation for skin care products. _____ **B** _____ the anti-wrinkle segment is still almost entirely comprised of a small but cash rich group of mature professionals, while the whitening segment is made up of a broad spectrum of youth and young adults. _____ **C** _____ there is a market for our whitening products among mature professionals. _____ **D** _____ , let's look at the customer profile of these two segments in more detail.

簡報片段 3

_____ **A** _____ sales results for the last three years contrasted with targets for the same period. _____ **B** _____ , results have been consistently down from targets across the period. _____ **C** _____ this. While you could argue that our sales teams are not meeting their targets, it is possible to suggest that targets — which are set by head office in the US — are unrealistic and do not reflect real local market conditions. _____ **D** _____ a comparison of sales and targets in other regions to see how we compare.

簡報片段 4

_____ **A** _____ costs and margins for our three main lines in all three markets. _____ **B** _____ there has been a consistent decline in the Easyloop brand in all three markets, while the other two key brands have grown. _____ **C** _____ the strategy the agency is using for this particular brand is not working for us. _____ **D** _____ , we can analyze these figures in slightly more detail.

| Word List |

segmentation 〔͵sɛgmən'teʃən〕 *n.* 區隔　　whitening 〔'hwaɪtənɪŋ〕 *n.* 美白

答案 建議各位將答案寫在另外一張紙上，如此，下次練習時可以使用不同的 set-phrases。也建議各位大聲朗讀這些簡報，口說練習比寫答案卷重要得多。攸關簡報成敗的是口說技巧，而非書寫技巧。也可以將自己的練習錄下來，聽聽看有無需要改進的部分。接著請核對答案。

簡報片段 1

 • I'd now like you to look at
 • If you look at this (chart/graph/table), you can see
 • If you look here you can see
 • On this slide we've got
 • These statistics show
 • This graph displays
 • This slide shows

B • As you can see,
 • I'd like to draw your attention to the fact that
 • Notice that
 • We can see from this graph that

C • it is clear from this (chart/graph/table/movement) that
 • it is clear from the general movement that
 • these figures suggest that
 • these statistics show that
 • this slide shows that

D • Let's turn now to ... which we can see here.

簡報片段 2

 • I'd now like you to look at
 • On this slide we've got

B • As you can see, ...
 • I'd like to draw your attention to the fact that
 • Look at the way that
 • Notice that
 • We can see from this graph that

C
- It is clear from this (chart/graph/table/movement) that
- It is clear from the general movement that
- These figures suggest that
- These statistics show
- This slide shows that

D
- Moving on to the next slide

簡報片段 3

A
- I'd now like you to look at
- If you look at this (chart/graph/table), you can see
- If you look here you can see
- On this slide we've got
- These statistics show
- This graph displays
- This slide describes
- This slide shows

B
- As you can see

C
- Let me elaborate on
- Let me expand on

D
- Let's turn to

簡報片段 4

A
- If you look at this (chart/graph/table), you can see
- If you look here you can see
- On this slide we've got
- These statistics show
- This graph displays
- This next slide gives us the figures for
- This slide shows

B
- I'd like to draw your attention to the fact that
- Look at the way that
- Notice that
- We can see from this graph that

C • It is clear from the general movement that
 • These figures suggest that
 • These statistics show that
D • Moving on to the next slide

接著，利用這些 set-phrases 來做一個口說練習。請做下一個 Task 。

Task 6.7

請看下圖。標上你所屬產業的相關資訊，並加上數字。決定你要突顯的資訊，以及你要如何摘要說明。練習以學過的 set-phrases 和四個程序來說明這個圖表。

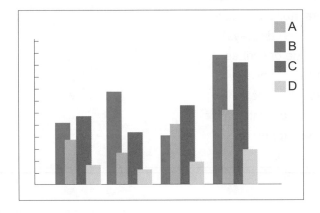

答案 可以將自己的練習錄下來以便評估。也可以利用最近在簡報中用過的圖表做一些額外的練習。

實戰要領：眼神接觸與肢體語言

除了聲音之外，還有兩個要素決定你的表現優劣：眼神接觸與肢體語言。請參考下表所列的「Do's」和「Don'ts」，仔細回想自己過去的表現。有個方法很值得一試，就是對著鏡子做上一個 Task，注意自己在眼神接觸和肢體語言方面有哪些是需要改進的。

下次聽別人簡報時，注意他們的眼神接觸和肢體語言。你能從他們的表現學到什麼？

眼神接觸

除了第二、三章中談到的聲音，第二個對簡報表現影響最大的因素就是眼神。眼神是你和觀眾交流、建立默契的方式之一，因此良好的眼神接觸是很重要的。

Do	Don't
直視觀眾眼睛。這有助於傳達想法，以及加強說服力。	不要老盯著觀眾頭頂上方。這樣做會顯得你很害羞。
環視每一位觀眾來加強語氣。不要漏掉任何一個人。	不要只盯著某個人看。這樣會使被注視的人感到緊張，也會讓其他人以為你是不是愛上他了！
如果一時忘詞了，就看一下筆記。	如果一時忘詞了，別盯著天花板看，這樣會顯得很茫然。

肢體語言

除了聲音和眼神接觸，姿勢與手勢也很重要，攸關觀眾對你進行簡報專業能力的信心。你得找出一個自在又好看的姿勢，再加上俐落、有力的手勢。試著在鏡子前面練習，直到能展現出自信與專業為止。

Do

對觀眾微笑。你看起來會很和善，
而且有自信。

Don't

別對著觀眾皺眉頭。你看起來會心
事重重，而且不易親近。

記住身體要自然地挺直，兩手自然
地擺放。

不要低頭垂肩或雙手交叉。這樣看
起來不易親近；也不要站得像個士
兵，觀眾會覺得很奇怪。

如果你穿的是褲了， 一隻手不妨插在口袋裡，這樣可以展現出自信。但記住用另一隻手作手勢。

不要兩隻手都插在口袋裡。這樣看起來過於隨便，會讓人反感；如果你一手放在口袋，不要把玩零錢或鑰匙。這樣會使觀眾分心。

如果使用麥克風，一手握住即可，另一手用來作手勢。（可在家用筆練習）

如果使用麥克風，記住不要讓麥克風擋住臉。

117

Do

面對觀眾。如果適當的話，也可以來回走動。

Don't

不要背對著觀眾：這樣他們不容易聽到你的聲音。

Do

找出一個自己覺得自在的姿勢，並不時換回這種姿勢。不要煩躁不安，這會讓觀眾質疑你是怎麼了。

Do

運用雙手作手勢。手裡握支筆或指示棒可能會讓你比較自在。如果不知雙手該往哪兒放也不必擔心。觀眾並不曉得你的感覺。

看過「眼神接觸」與「肢體語言」的要領後,可以回頭複習前面章節的「實戰要領」單元,然後再做一遍先前的 Task 。特別建議各位做引言的練習,因為這攸關觀眾對你的信心。在進行接下來章節中的練習時,不要忘了這些學過的技巧。

在進入下一個章節之前,請回頭看看本章的「學習目標」,你達成了多少?如果還有不清楚的部分,就再複習一次。

UNIT 7

描述「改變」的用語

achieving
success

引言與學習目標

上一個章節介紹了使用視覺材料的四個程序。其中的用語適用於架構投影片的說明，與強調相關的資訊。本章中介紹的用語則是用於說明投影片的內容。

還記得在第五章中提到的架構與內容視覺材料嗎？內容視覺材料應該用來說明某種「改變」，例如：銷售成長或下滑、營運成本或市佔率的改變、公司與主要競爭對手之間的績效比較、目標與成果之間的差距等。本章介紹的用語就是用來描述這些改變。

看完本章，你應該達到的學習目標如下：

❑ 能使用許多不同的動詞來描述變化。
❑ 對於完成與未完成式時態的意義和重要性有清楚的了解。
❑ 針對本章中的動詞做聽力練習。
❑ 針對本章中的動詞做發音練習。
❑ 學會用許多動詞來說明與安排簡報中的資訊。

簡報中的動詞時態

　　首先來談談「時間」。在簡報中使用視覺資料說明變化時，可能是指一段已完成或過去時間的變化，也可能是一段未完成或現在時間的改變。有時候也會談到未來的改變，但這情況比較簡單，只要用 will 即可。接著，先探討已完成和未完成期間的相關用語。為了確保各位了解我的意思，請先做下一個 Task 。

Task 7.1

請看下列的 time chunks 。將它們分類填入下面正確的欄位。見範例。

1. this year
2. last year
3. last quarter
4. during that time
5. during this time
6. ago
7. in September
8. until now

9. year-to-date
10. yesterday
11. this week
12. this quarter
13. then
14. in 1999
15. so far

現在時間的 Chunks Present (Unfinished) Time Chunks	過去時間的 Chunks Past (Finished) Time Chunks
• this year	

答案 ▌請以下列的必備語庫檢查答案。

簡報必備語庫 7.1

現在時間的 Chunks Present (Unfinished) Time Chunks	過去時間的 Chunks Past (Finished) Time Chunks
• this year • during this time • year-to-date • this week • this quarter • so far • until now	• last year • last quarter • during that time • ago • in September • yesterday • then • in 1999

★ 📂 語庫小叮嚀

◆ Year-to-date 「從年初到現在」，指的是未完成的一段時間。

◆ 「in + 月份」通常是指過去的時間，例：In September ，如果是在九月份做簡報，就不能說 in September ，而應該說 this month 。 In September 也可以用來談論未來。

◆ 「in + 年份」通常是指過去的時間。如果你想談的是今年，應該用 this year 。

◆ 注意，表示年份時的說法是 in 1999 或 in 2003 ，而不是 in year 1999 或 in year 2003 。大家都知道你指的是年份，所以不須再用 year 這個字了。

　　現在應該對已完成和未完成有一個清楚的概念了，接著來做一個聽力練習，請做下一個 Task 。

Task 7.2

Track 7.1 & 7.2

請聽 Track 7.1 和 7.2 ，並回答下列問題：

1. 每個簡報片段各是屬於何種時間？

2. 你是依據什麼來作判斷的？

答案 1. Track 7.1 ：未完成或現在的時間； Track 7.2 ：已完成或過去的時間。
2. 如果你預期在 Tracks 裡聽到關於時間的字眼，你可能會覺得這個練習蠻難的，因為根本就沒有關於時間的字眼！其實判斷屬於何種時間的關鍵都被藏在動詞裡頭。如果你還有點困惑，繼續研讀本章吧。

中文與英文的差別在於：在中文裡，關於時間的資訊是以如 Task 7.1 中的 time chunks 來表示；但在英文裡，時間的資訊是以動詞時態來表達，但中文的動詞並沒有時態。因此，當你在閱讀英文或是聽其他人說英文時，注意時態是很重要的。

簡報中談到已完成的過去期間，就應該使用過去簡單式（simple past tense）。如果是談到未完成的現在期間，就得用現在完成式（present perfect tense）。這個概念非常重要。請看下表，有助於理解。

已完成的過去時間：過去式 Finished Time Periods – the Past	未完成的現在時間：現在式 Unfinished Time Periods – the Present
過去簡單式： V-ed 或不規則動詞的過去式	現在完成式： have + p.p.

再聽一遍剛剛的簡報片段，這次應該更能抓到要點。請做下一個 Task 。如果覺得難，可以多聽幾次，但不要先看錄音稿。

Task 7.3

 Track 7.1 & 7.2

請再聽一次 Track 7.1 和 7.2 。將聽到的動詞記下來。記住動詞要以正確的時態寫出來。

答案 **Track 7.1**
- have increased
- have remained steady
- have been switching

Track 7.2
- did not match
- were unevenly distributed
- achieved

- were
- 你也許寫下了一些 set-phrases 中的動詞,如: draw、see。這些動詞有些不同,因為它們是從上一章說明視覺材料的 set-phrases 而來,它們不是簡報內容的動詞,現在只要注意內容的動詞。
- 從時態可看出來 Track 7.1 是屬於未完成或現在時間,而 Track 7.2 則是已完成或過去的時間。
- 如果有疑惑,建議你翻到書末附錄的錄音稿,將 Track 7.1 和 7.2 所有的內容動詞標出來。也可以將前一章的 set-phrases 劃出來作為複習。

描述「改變」的動詞

　　各位對時間以及如何使用時態有了進一步的認識後，現在再來看一些描述改變的動詞。請做下面的 Task，在完成之前不要先看答案。

Task 7.4

將下列描述改變的動詞分類。見範例。

1. decreased
2. dropped
3. fell
4. has/have decreased
5. has/have fallen
6. has/have gone down
7. has/have gone up
8. has/have increased
9. has/have remained constant
10. has/have remained steady
11. has/have risen
12. has/have stabilized
13. have/has dropped

14. have/has rocketed
15. have/has shot up
16. have/has surged
17. increased
18. remained constant
19. remained steady
20. rocketed
21. rose
22. shot up
23. stabilized
24. surged
25. went down
26. went up

| Word List |

rocket〔ˋrɑkɪt〕v. 猛漲　　　　　　　　　shoot up 驟升
surge〔sɝdʒ〕v. 高漲；驟增

	完成的時間 Finished Time	未完成的時間 Unfinished Time
向上的動作 **Movement** **Up**		
向下的動作 **Movement** **Down**	• decreased	
輕微的動作 **Very Little Movement**		

答案 ▌請以必備語庫 7.2 核對答案。

簡報必備語庫 7.2

	完成的時間 Finished Time	未完成的時間 Unfinished Time
向上的動作 **Movement Up**	• increased • rose • went up • shot up • rocketed • surged	• has/have increased • has/have risen • has/have gone up • has/have shot up • has/have rocketed • has/have surged
向下的動作 **Movement Down**	• decreased • fell • went down • dropped	• has/have decreased • has/have fallen • has/have gone down • has/have dropped
輕微的動作 **Very Little Movement**	• remained constant • remained steady • stabilized	• has/have remained constant • has/have remained steady • has/have stabilized

接著來練習這些動詞的發音。請做下面的 Task 。注意簡單過去式的 ed 如何發音（如：dropped 、 decreased），以及現在完成式中的動詞 have 和 has 如何發音。記住，熟能生巧。

Task 7.5

 Track 7.3

邊聽邊複誦 Track 7.3 ，練習這些動詞的發音。

接著配合前後文來練習這些動詞，這樣才能真正了解這兩種時態的差別，以及如何使用。請做下一個 Task 。你得先研究下列表格，並把內文多看幾遍，這個 Task 可不簡單喔！

Task 7.6

參考下頁表格所提供的資訊，由必備語庫 7.2 中選出適當的動詞填入下列空格。記住使用正確的時態。

So far this year, profits _____ **A** _____ steadily, despite our best efforts to increase sales. In the first quarter, sales _____ **B** _____ slowly, but in the second quarter, they _____ **C** _____ quickly. In Q$_3$, they _____ **D** _____ and we are hopeful that they will start to move up again in the last quarter.
The situation has worsened due to the fact that during the same period production costs _____ **E** _____ .

If we look at last year's figures, we can see a trend. In the third quarter, sales _____ **F** _____ slowly, but _____ **G** _____ to the Q$_1$ level in Q$_4$.

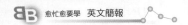
TABLE

	Last Year				This Year			
	Q₁	Q₂	Q₃	Q₄	Q₁	Q₂	Q₃	Q₄
profits $m	4.6	4.4	4.2	5	4.8	4.7	4.6	
sales 1,000s	10	9	8	10	9.5	7.7	7.68	
costs $m	1.8	1.9	2	2.1	2.2	2.3	2.4	

答案 | 記住，使用 have 或 has 得視主詞為單數或複數來決定，相信這點你已經知道了！

A
- have decreased
- have fallen
- have gone down

B
- decreased
- went down
- fell

C
- decreased
- went down
- fell

D
- have remained constant
- have remained steady

E
- have gone up
- have increased
- have risen

F
- decreased
- fell
- went down

G
- increased
- rose
- went up

　　對如何運用描述變化的動詞有了基本概念後,接下來的重點就是不斷練習,直到可以在簡報中應用自如。下一個 Task 需要多演練幾次,直到可以熟練地說明視覺材料,而不會結結巴巴。

Task 7.7　　　　　　　　　　　　　　　　　　　　　　Track 7.4

請說明下圖(你目前是在 Q₄)。

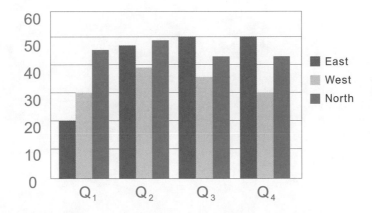

答案　利用這個圖表多練習幾次,可以加入上一章中的 set-phrases。練習完後,再聽 Track 7.4 中使用這個圖表的範例,也可參看書末的錄音稿。

Task 7.8

再次說明 Task 7.7 中的圖表,這次要連上一章的 set-phrases 一起運用。

答案　從書末的錄音稿中可看出，主講者並未提出任何數據，只是專注在一般的變化上。也許這位主講者是企圖為他們的區域多爭取一位銷售人員。你能否看出她是如何設計簡報以達到此目的？

語感甦活區：簡報中的關鍵動詞

在「語感甦活區」這一節要介紹一些非常重要的動詞，用來說明簡報正在進行的工作，或是針對提出的資訊做評論。請看以下句子：

- I'd like to point out here that these figures are not complete.
  我要指出一點，這些數據並不完整。
- We need to examine the reasons for this failure in more detail.
  我們得更仔細地檢討失敗的原因。

以上二個例句，主講者是在說明某些訊息。

- Let's turn now to the financials.
  我們現在來看財務狀況。
- I'd like to conclude by going over the main points again.
  我要再次重複這些要點以做個結束。

以上兩個例句，主講者是在組織訊息。

現在請做下一個 Task 。

Task 7.9

請看下列簡報中常見的動詞，並練習造句。

描述訊息 Describing Information	組織訊息 Structuring Information
• consider n.p. • address the issue of n.p. • show you 'wh' + n. clause • show you n.p. • discuss n.p. • discuss 'wh' + n. clause • point out n.p. • point out that + n. clause • mention sth. • mention that + n. clause • talk about n.p. • tell you about n.p. • look at n.p. • look at the way + n. clause • describe 'wh' + n. clause • describe n.p. • examine n.p. • consider 'wh' + n. clause	• turn to n.p. • go on to n.p. • go on to V • conclude by Ving

答案 這些動詞可以用來說明或是組織你想傳達的資訊。

- I'd now like to address the issue of increasing production costs.
  我現在要談到是生產成本增加這個議題。
- Let's turn now to revenue for the last 5 years.
  現在來看看過去五年來的盈收。
- I'm going to be examining the results from our competitors to show what we're missing out on.
  我將檢視我們競爭者的成果，看看我們錯失了什麼。

可以回到第三章，看看簡報必備語庫 3.1 的小叮嚀，複習關於替換 set-phrases 中現在動詞的建議。也可利用上述的部分動詞來練習那些 set-phrases。

好了，本章到此結束，這也是簡報主體部分的尾聲。下個章節會開始介紹簡報的結尾。進入下個章節之前，請先回到本章的「學習目標」，看看你達成了多少？

PART 3

簡報的總結

UNIT
8

總結

achieving
success

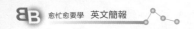
引言與學習目標

　　接下來的二章介紹的是簡報的總結部分。本章介紹如何結束簡報，下一章則談論 Q&A 的部分。

　　如同簡報的引言，觀眾也會記住總結的部分。這是你確認訊息清楚傳達、以及達成目的的最後機會。

　　簡報的總結非常重要，所以需要費心設計。簡報進行到結尾時，許多觀眾可能都已昏昏欲睡，所以得把他們喚醒、告知簡報即將進入尾聲，並且以適當的方式結束讓大家留下深刻的印象。這個章節即是介紹結束簡報的適當方式、讓觀眾留下深刻印象的結語 set-phrases 、以及有助於簡報表現的實用技巧。研讀完本章，你應該達到的學習目標如下：

　　❑ 了解簡報總結的四步驟並能靈活運用。
　　❑ 學會結語的 set-phrases 。
　　❑ 練習聽力與發音。
　　❑ 學會簡報實用的關鍵名詞。

總結的四步驟

首先，先做個聽力練習。不要先看錄音稿哦。

Task 8.1

 Track 8.1

請聽 Track 8.1 中簡報總結的片段。這些片段有何共通點？

答案
- 結構相同。希望你能聽出各主講者在組織總結時的相似處，稍後會詳細地介紹總結的結構。
- 所有的主講者都在總結時放慢說話速度。

剛剛聽到的所有簡報都是依循相同的四步驟設計的。首先，主講者提醒觀眾簡報即將進入總結；第二步，總結要點，或重申重要結論；第三，感謝觀眾；最後，請觀眾提出問題。總結各點如下：

總結的四步驟

Step 1 ：告知觀眾簡報接近尾聲。
Step 2 ：結論／總結要點。
Step 3 ：感謝觀眾。
Step 4 ：請觀眾提問。

Task 8.2

 Track 8.1

請重聽 Track 8.1 中的所有簡報片段，看看是否能聽出上述的四個步驟。

答案
希望各位都能聽得出這四個步驟，如果不行也不用擔心，繼續做下一個 Task 。等學過下列的用語之後，你會覺得簡單許多。

接著來看看主講者所使用的用語。請做下一個 Task 。

Task 8.3

將這些 set-phrases 分類並填入下表。

1. At this point, I'd be very interested to hear your questions or any comments you may have.
2. I think it's clear that we should V ...
3. I'd like to end by Ving ...
4. I'd like to end with n.p. ...
5. In conclusion, I would like to suggest that + n. clause
6. In conclusion, I think we need to V ...
7. In conclusion, I think we should V ...
8. In conclusion, I would like to recommend that + n. clause
9. Now I would like to invite you to ask any questions you may have.
10. OK, now you are welcome to ask any questions.
11. The key issue is whether + n. clause
12. OK, that ends the main part of my presentation to you today.
13. Right then, are there any questions?
14. So, any questions?
15. So, let's just summarize the main points.
16. So, to wind up, I think we should V ...
17. Thanks, everyone.
18. Thank you for listening and for inviting me here today.
19. Thank you for your attention.
20. Thanks for listening.
21. That concludes my presentation today.
22. There are two recommendations I would like to make at this point.
23. OK, I think that just about covers it.
24. I'd like to end by summarizing ...
25. I think I'll stop here.

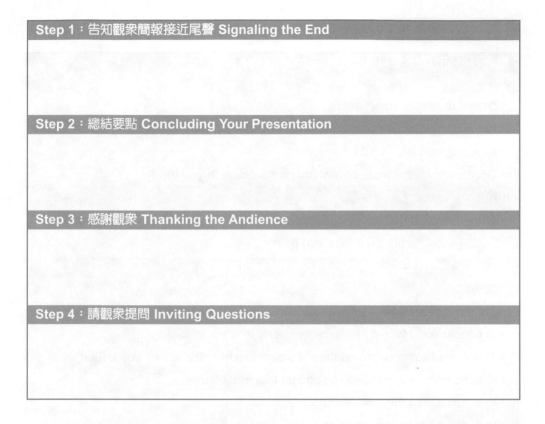

Step 1：告知觀眾簡報接近尾聲 Signaling the End

Step 2：總結要點 Concluding Your Presentation

Step 3：感謝觀眾 Thanking the Andience

Step 4：請觀眾提問 Inviting Questions

接著請先做下一個 Task，然後再看答案。

Task 8.4

再看一遍 Task 8.3 中的 set-phrases，哪些 set-phrases 會在正式的簡報中使用，哪些又會在非正式的簡報中使用？

答案 請以必備語庫 8.1 核對答案。正式與非正式用語之間會有部分重疊。在不同的簡報場合該用何種 set-phrases，可由各位對觀眾的了解以及簡報的目的來判斷。

簡報必備語庫 8.1

Step 1：告知觀眾簡報接近尾聲 Signaling the End

Formal

- I'd like to end by summarizing ...
- I'd like to end by Ving ...
- I'd like to end with n.p. ...
- OK, that ends the main part of my presentation to you today.

Informal

- OK, I think that just about covers it.
- So, let's just summarize the main points.

Step 2：總結要點 Concluding Your Presentation

Formal

- The key issue is whether + n. clause
- In conclusion, I would like to recommend that + n. clause
- There are two recommendations I would like to make at this point. First, ...
- In conclusion, I would like to suggest that + n. clause
- In conclusion, I think we should V ...
- In conclusion, I think we need to V ...
- That concludes my presentation to you today.
- I think it's clear that we should V ...

Informal

- So, to wind up, I think we should V ...
- I think I'll stop here.

Step 3：感謝觀眾 Thanking the Audience

Formal

- Thank you for your attention.
- Thank you for listening and for inviting me here today.

Informal

- Thanks, everyone.
- Thanks for listening.

Step 4 ：請觀眾提問 Inviting Questions

Formal

• Now I would like to invite you to ask any questions you may have.

• At this point, I'd be very interested to hear your questions or any comments you may have.

Informal

• So, any questions?

• Right then, are there any questions?

• OK, now you are welcome to ask any questions.

Task 8.5　　　　　　　　　　　　　　　　　　Track 8.1

請聽 Track 8.1 的第一個簡報片段，勾選出你聽到的 set-phrases 。

答案｜ • 可翻至書末的錄音稿，核對答案。
　　　 • 注意 set-phrases 和句子連結的方式。
　　　 • 注意音調和連音的特徵，這對於發音練習很有幫助。

Task 8.6　　　　　　　　　　　　　　　　　　Track 8.2

請聽 Track 8.2 練習語庫中 set-phrases 的發音。

答案｜ 花二十分鐘做這個練習。記住，練習時不要看 set-phrases ，專注在聽力與記憶力上。每個 set-phrases 練習五遍以上之後，再看一遍語庫，挑出你覺得需要加強的部分，不斷練習直到你有信心為止。

　　接著來練習運用這些 set-phrases 。

Task 8.7

請由語庫中挑選適當的 set-phrases ，填入下列空格。

_____ **Ⓐ** _____ the main point of my presentation. _____ **Ⓑ** _____ adjust our pricing strategy to try to boost sales. I have outlined the arguments against doing so, as well as why I think we should. We have seen the result of a pricing readjustment in our competitors' sales, and while I am not suggesting we enter into a price war, _____ **Ⓒ** _____ we take advantage of the slight reduction in production costs to lower our prices. _____ **Ⓓ** _____ _____ **Ⓔ** _____

答案 建議各位大聲朗讀簡報片段，並在朗誦時即時插入 set-phrases，藉以練習 set-phrase 和內容之間的轉換。口說的練習比寫答案卷有用得多。攸關簡報成敗的是口說技巧，而非書寫技巧。可將練習錄下來，聽聽有無需要改進的地方。核對下列答案。

Ⓐ
- I'd like to end with
- I'd like to end by summarizing

Ⓑ
- The key issue is whether we should
- In conclusion, I think we should
- In conclusion, I think we need to
- I think it's clear that we should

Ⓒ
- in conclusion, I would like to recommend that
- in conclusion, I would like to suggest that

Ⓓ
- Thank you for your attention.
- Thank you for listening and for inviting me here today.
- Thanks, everyone.
- Thanks for listening.

Ⓔ
- Now I would like to invite you to ask any questions you may have.
- At this point, I'd be very interested to hear any questions or comments you may have.
- OK, now you are welcome to ask any questions.

簡報的總結必須讓人印象深刻，所以須要多多練習，請再做下一個 Task 。

Task 8.8

請由語庫中挑選適當的 set-phrases ，填入下列空格。

_____**A**_____ _____**B**_____ change the campaign strategy to appeal to the middle segment of the market where we can expect more growth. Based on the market research I have shown you, I am confident that adjusting our strategy in this way will give us the sales figures we need to meet our targets and be the best in the region. _____**C**_____

_____**D**_____

答案 下列的參考答案都是較非正式的 set-phrases ，但若你選用的是較正式的 set-phrases 也無妨。在練習大聲朗讀時，也應該練習放慢速度，但是要維持聲音的強度。記住要運用聲音來標示轉折。可以多聽幾遍 CD ，看看主講者是怎麼做的。

核對下列答案。

A
- OK, that ends the main part of my presentation to you today.
- OK, I think that just about covers it.
- So, let's just summarize the main points.

B
- In conclusion, I would like to recommend that (we)
- In conclusion, I would like to suggest that (we)
- In conclusion, I think we should
- In conclusion, I think we need to
- I think it's clear that we should
- So, to wind up, I think we should

C
- Thank you for your attention.
- Thank you for listening and for inviting me here today.
- Thanks, everyone.
- Thanks for listening.

D • So, any questions?
 • Right then, are there any questions?
 • OK, now you are welcome to ask any questions.

Task 8.9

請利用本章的 set-phrases 和四個步驟來設計自己的簡報總結。並運用先前所學過的聲音技巧來練習，直到有信心能讓觀眾留下深刻印象為止。

語感甦活區：簡報中的關鍵名詞

這部分要介紹的是簡報中的一些關鍵名詞。請看下列這個 set-phrase ：

• The key issue is whether ...
關鍵議題為是否……

這個 set-phrase 的關鍵名詞是 issue「議題」加上前面的形容詞。 Issue 這個字非常實用，因為它很抽象，可用來指你要提出的「主題」或「要點」。下面列出這類名詞，以及經常搭配使用的形容詞。

請做下面的 Task 。

Task 8.10

請看下表的 word partnership 並練習造句。

形容詞		名詞
• obvious	• underlying	
• fundamental	• important	
• real	• major	
• recurrent	• specific	i s s u e
• contentious	• critical	
• key	• central	
• controversial	• core	

| Word List |

recurrent〔rɪˋkɝ-ənt〕*adj.* 一再發生的   contentious〔kənˋtɛnʃəs〕*adj.* 有爭議的

答案 ▌第一句是簡報引言中陳述目的的句子；第二、三句屬於總結的部分；最後兩句屬於問答的部分，在下一章會更深入討論。

- The underlying issue I will be addressing is the need for tighter system controls.
  我要討論的基本議題是對於更嚴格系統管控的需求。
- The key issue is whether we should adjust our strategy.
  主要的議題是我們是否應該修正我們的策略。
- The fundamental issue is whether we should adjust our strategy.
  基本的議題是我們是否應該修正我們的策略。
- That's a very contentious issue. What do you think?
  這個議題十分地有爭議性。你的看法如何？

Task 8.11

請看下表的 word partnership 並練習造句。

形容詞		名詞
• serious	• initial	
• vital	• greatest	
• primary	• legitimate	concern
• central	• principle	
• important	• key	

答案 ▌第一句是簡報引言中陳述目的的句子；第二、三句屬於總結的部分；最後兩句屬於問答的部分，在下一章會更深入討論。

- The problem with cash-flow is obviously one of our most serious concerns.
  現金流量的問題是我們擔憂的問題中最嚴重的。

Word List

legitimate〔lɪ`dʒɪtəmɪt〕 adj. 真正的；合法的

- The key concern is whether we should adjust our strategy.
  主要的顧慮是我們是否應該調整我們的策略。
- The central concern is whether we should adjust our strategy.
  主要的顧慮是我們是否應該調整我們的策略。
- This is one of our key concerns.
  這是我們主要的顧慮之一。
- You've raised a legitimate concern there.
  你提出了一個合理的問題。

進入下一章 Q&A 之前，回到本章的「學習目標」，看看你達成了多少？

UNIT 9

問答

achieving
success

引言與學習目標

這一章要討論的是簡報最令人害怕的部分： Q&A 。許多人覺得這個部分就像考試一樣恐怖。

首先必須告訴各位： Q&A 並非考試。如果準備充分、熟記資料，也清楚自己的目的，這個部分就應該不會有問題。只要能聽懂題目，應該就能回答出關於簡報內容的問題，稍後會細談這個部分。這個章節的主要目的是改變大家對 Q&A 的看法，應該要以正面的角度來看 Q&A 。就我而言，整個簡報中我最喜歡這個部分，因為這是和觀眾溝通的最後一個機會，也是達成目的的最後一次機會。

研讀完本章，你應該達到的學習目標如下：

❏ 學會一些回答棘手問題的對策。
❏ 學會一些 Q&A 中用到的 set-phrases 。
❏ 改變對 Q&A 的看法。
❏ 針對一些不同種類的問題做聽力練習。

Q&A 的種類及對策

先來看看一般人會害怕 Q&A 的原因。

Task 9.1

列舉一些你認為 Q&A 非常困難的原因。

答案 下面列舉出一些可能的原因，哪些和你的感覺最接近？

1. 問答部分我有信心可以應付自如。

   ➡ 如果有信心應付這個部分，恭喜！你可以跳過本章節！

2. 因為無法預測觀眾會問哪些問題，所以不知該準備哪些 set-phrases 和 word partnerships 。萬一想說的字說不出來，怎麼辦？

   ➡ 如果準備足夠，對簡報主題也有充分了解（做簡報本來就應該充分了解主題！），應該就不用擔心。稍後也會介紹一些這個部分會用到的 set-phrases 。

3. 有時候聽不懂發問者的英文，請他們重複一次問題又讓我覺得過意不去。

   ➡ 聽不懂發問者的英文不需覺得過意不去。是誰在說讓人聽不懂的英文？他們的發音不好，不是你的錯呀！

4. 我覺得每個問題都是挑戰。

   ➡ 這是因為事前的準備不夠充分。記得先前提到的嗎？熟記你的資料，如果充分了解資料，絕對可以應付任何問題。

5. 有一些觀眾似乎想要踢館，盡問一些不相干的問題。

   ➡ 不要讓這樣的事發生。身為主講者，應該主導你的簡報、規範觀眾的提問。不須上演全武行，只要微笑（讓他們不好意思），並問他們這個問題和主題有什麼關聯即可。

總言之，不妨將 Q&A 當作是一個辯論的機會，而不是一個測驗。

依我的經驗， Q&A 的問題可分為三大類：

1. Questions you know you <u>can</u> answer
   確定自己會回答的問題。
2. Questions you're <u>not sure</u> you can answer
   <u>不確定</u>自己是否會回答的問題。
3. Questions you know you <u>cannot</u> answer
   確定自己<u>不會</u>回答的問題。

針對每一類問題，你得想出一個對策以及一些用語。首先來討論問題的對策。

1. 確定會回答的問題。
對策：先謝謝觀眾提出這個問題，然後再回答。回答時，看著發問者的眼睛，面帶微
笑，藉此與對方有直接的交流。但是在回答的過程中不要忽略了其他觀眾。

2. 不確定是否會回答的問題。
　　不確定是否會回答有幾個原因：第一，不確定是否聽懂了發問者的英文；第二，
可能聽懂了他的英文，但不確定問題的重點在哪；第三，聽懂問題，但不確定如何回
答。
對策：不論是哪種原因，都請觀眾重複一次問題，如此一來，不僅可以聽懂他的問
題，<u>也</u>可爭取時間思考如何回答。

3. 確定不會回答的問題。
　　確定不會回答有幾個原因：第一，不能透露這個資訊；第二，手邊沒有這筆資
料；第三，思考了這個問題，但還是不了解問題的重點、或不知該怎麼回答。
對策：不論是哪種原因，你應該有技巧地迴避回答，但不要讓觀眾覺得你在迴避問
題。

　　不論是回答哪一類問題，態度和表現方式都應保持自信與專業。來做一些聽力練
習，你是否能聽出主講者回答每一類問題時是採取哪種策略？請做 Task 9.2 。

Task 9.2　　　　　　　　　　　　　　　　　　　　　　　Track 9.1

請聽 Track 9.1 ，判斷你聽到的問題分別被主講者歸為哪一類，以及主講者採用了何種策
略來回答？見範例。

Q1：　第二類：不確定是否會回答的問題。_____

Q2：_____

Q3：_____

Q4：_____

Q5：_____

Q6：_____

Q7：_____

答案　**Q1**：第二類
對策：主講者請發問者先說說自己的意見。如果不太確定要如何回答，這是個不錯的策略，因為主講者可直接對發問者的意見做回應，有時甚至只須回應說：Yes, that's entirely my view of the matter. Any more questions?「沒錯，那正是我對這個問題的看法，還有其他問題嗎？」

Q2：第一類
對策：主講者先謝謝這位觀眾提問，然後直接回答。

Q3：第三類
對策：主講者認為這個問題與主題無關，也可能因為主講者對來自日本的競爭並不了解，也可能是她刻意將簡報的重點放在中國。注意，她是以堅定但有禮的方式回絕這個問題。

Q4：第三類
對策：主講者並未回答問題，但卻利用這個機會重申在開場時所陳述的目的 —— 說服團隊多費心經營本地的短期目標，而將區域的長期計劃留給總公司去傷腦筋。發問者或其他觀眾可能不會注意到主講者並沒有真正回答問題。因為我們都很容易被「預期」誤導，也就是說，如果提出了一個問題，就一定有人回答，即使問題並<u>沒有</u>被回答，我們還是<u>覺得</u>得到了答案。這雖然是政客玩的老把戲，但在簡報中如果遇到不知如何回答的問題，這招仍是非常管用。找朋友來練習練習，看看他們是否注意到什麼端倪。

Q5：第二類
對策：這裡的問題出在，發問者的發音和英文程度使主講者很難理解問題。注意

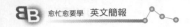
主講者如何以自己的方式重複一次問題。希望發問者會因為自己的破英文而不好意思再多說什麼。

Q6：第一類

對策：主講者首先謝謝發問者提出了一個好問題。這個舉動會讓發問者感到窩心，主講者也得以展現自信與專業。

Q7：第二類

對策：主講者在拖延時間，因為她還不確定要如何回答。注意主講者拖延時間的方式，她一面慢條斯理地評論這個問題，一面思考要如何回答。

　　如果你的答案和上列答案出入頗大，請再練習一次。這個 Task 也許有點難，但希望你能查覺到主講者回答問題的表現、聲音、聲調與時機的掌握都非常專業！

應答的 Set-phrases

看過了應付難題的對策，繼續來看看有哪些用語可以派上用場。請做下一個 Task 。

Task 9.3

將下列的 set-phrases 分類並填入下表。

1. Can I get back to you on that one?
2. Could I deal with that later? Thanks.
3. Hmm. Yes. Interesting point. What do you think?
4. I don't know without seeing the figures.
5. I haven't seen the data on this, so I'm not in a position to give you a clear answer yet.
6. I'm afraid I simply don't know.
7. I'm glad you asked me. I think ...
8. I'm not sure I can answer that at this time.
9. I'm not sure I follow. Do you mean ...?
10. Perhaps you could write to me with your question.
11. I think that's a legitimate concern.
12. You've raised a contentious issue there.
13. Thanks for that question. In my opinion ...
14. To be honest, I think that raises a different issue.
15. Well, I think I answered that earlier, but to repeat, ...
16. Well, you've raised a very interesting point there. In reply I would like to point out that ...
17. Yes, good point. I think ...
18. Yes, I see. What are your views on this before I give my own?
19. Yes, I understand. As I mentioned earlier, I think ...
20. Yes, that's a very good question. It depends on 'wh' ...

21. You're right on the money! That's exactly what I thought.

22. I'm afraid I can't comment on that.

23. I don't know the answer to your question, but I'll make a note here.

24. Thank you for pointing out the mistake here. I'm afraid it's a typo. The correct figure is ...

確定會回答的問題　Questions you know you can answer

不確定會回答的問題　Questions you're not sure you can answer

確定不會回答的問題　Questions you know you cannot answer

答案　請以下列必備語庫 9.1 核對答案。

- 第一類「確定會回答的問題」中的 set-phrases 是由二個部分組成。第一部分先評論問題，或謝謝發問者提問。第二部分則是回答問題。這二部分可以混搭使用。

- 第二類「不確定是否會回答的問題」。上一章的「語感甦活區」中，word partnership 表中的名詞和形容詞可以派上用場了。練習以不同的組合使用這些 set-phrases。

- 第三類「確定不會回答的問題」。 I'm afraid I simply don't know. 這個 set-phrase 只有在碰到非常棘手的問題時才會使用，語氣要堅定有禮，這樣才無損你的專業形象。沒有人規定你非得回答所有的問題不可——記住，這不是考試！不過話說回來，你也不能每次都用這句話來搪塞吧！

160

簡報必備語庫 9.1

確定會回答的問題　Questions you know you can answer

- Yes, good point. I think ...
- Thanks for that question. In my opinion ...
- Yes, I understand. As I mentioned earlier, I think ...
- Yes, that's a very good question. It depends on 'wh' ...
- Well, I think I answered that earlier, but to repeat, ...
- I'm glad you asked me. I think ...
- You're right on the money! That's exactly what I thought.
- Thank you for pointing out the mistake here. I'm afraid it's a typo. The correct figure is ...

不確定會回答的問題　Questions you're not sure you can answer

- You've raised a contentious issue there.
- Hmm. Yes. Interesting point. What do you think?
- Yes, I see. What are your views on this before I give my own?
- I'm not sure I follow. Do you mean ...?
- Well, you've raised a very interesting point there. In reply I would like to point out that ...
- To be honest, I think that raises a different issue.
- I think that's a legitimate concern.

確定不會回答的問題　Questions you know you cannot answer

- I'm not sure I can answer that at this time.
- I'm afraid I simply don't know.
- I haven't seen the data on this, so I'm not in a position to give you a clear answer yet.
- Could I deal with that later? Thanks.
- Can I get back to you on that one?
- Perhaps you could write to me with your question.
- I don't know without seeing the figures.
- I'm afraid I can't comment on that.
- I don't know the answer to your question, but I'll make a note here.

練習發音之前，先做下一個 Task 。

Task 9.4

請再聽一次 Track 9.1 ，其中運用了語庫 9.1 的哪些 set-phrases ？請勾選出來。注意連音和聲調的部分，以及主講者如何回應每個提問者。

答案 ▌請翻至書末附錄的錄音稿，看看主講者運用了哪些 set-phrases 。

接著來練習發音吧。

Task 9.5

請聽 Track 9.2 練習 set-phrases 的發音。

答案 ▌花二十分鐘做這個練習。記住，練習時不要看 set-phrases ，專注在聽力與記憶力上。每個 set-phrase 練習五遍後，再看一次語庫，挑選出須要加強的部分，然後不斷練習直到有信心為止。

　　本章最後一個 Task 要讓各位演練一些應付問題的 set-phrases 。我希望各個領域的專業人士都可以使用這本書，但要設計出各個領域能回答與不能回答的問題實在有其困難。所以，請各位想像一個情境：你剛完成了一場簡報，簡報的主題是：Presenting in English: how is it different from presenting in your own language?，目的是要說服觀眾用英文 prepare 、 practice 和 perform 簡報，接著你就要回答和主題相關的問題了。

　　在聽 Track 9.3 的問題時，儘可能很快地用記憶中的 set-phrases 來回答。訓練自己能迅速地對題目作出反應。

Task 9.6

請聽 Track 9.3 中的問題，用本章介紹的對策和 set-phrases 來回答。

答案
- 這個練習很難！希望各位能苦中作樂、多練習幾次，直到能很快地反應出該用哪些 set-phrases 。
- 不過一天別練習太多次。可以隔幾天再來練習，才不至於對問題太過於熟悉。這些問題應該要讓你有點驚訝，就像真實的 Q&A 一樣。
- 你可能會想以不同的方式來回答，在策略和 set-phrases 上做些變化，你不妨多複習一下本書。

　　在 prepare 和 practice 自己的簡報時，複習一下本章的 set-phrases ，你才能隨心地運用到簡報的 Q&A 中。

實戰要領：準備、操練、演出

用非母語進行簡報需要不同於母語的 prepare、practice、以及 perform 的程序、策略和技巧。主要原因是在於使用外國語言的困難度。因在說英文時，你得在 accuracy「精確度」和 fluency「流利度」之間做選擇。只有英文程度非常高的人才有能力在兩者間取得平衡。

假設說英文的過程如下圖：

圖 1

有時候你可以說得比較流利──在簡報熟悉的題目時，還有在輕鬆的情況下，你不用擔心文法或字彙出錯，這時你的口說狀況有如下圖：

圖 2

在某些情況下，你的心情無法放輕鬆，又碰到困難或不熟的題目，這時你就得顧全 accuracy，而慢條斯理地表達，你的口說狀況就會如下圖：

圖 3

在簡報的過程中，為了強化專業形象與增加達成目標的機率，你會想要在 fluency 和 accuracy 間取得平衡。要做到這點最好的方法就是：在 prepare 、 practice 和 perform 的過程中，以如下的圖示來進行：

圖4 準備

在準備階段（圖 4）專注在 accuracy 上。確實將 set-phrases 填入第四章中介紹的「簡報準備表」，並確認 word partnerships 正確無誤，你得用到的專業、艱澀用語也必須是正確的。

圖5 操練

在操練階段（圖 5），應該以 fluency 為目標，但 accuracy 還是必須保持。用錄音機來協助練習會很有幫助。

圖6 演出

accuracy
精確地

fluency
流暢地

在演出階段（圖 6），目標應該是 fluency 。觀眾不會知道你背後花了多少時間練習，但他們看到的會是流暢、自信、令人印象深刻的表現。整個練習過程的目標應該是：獲得更佳的 fluency ，但又不失 accuracy 。

本章結束前，請回頭看看「學習目標」，你達成了多少呢？

本書到此即將告一段落，在「結語」中還會介紹一些方法，教大家如何讓英文不斷地進步。

結 語

要跟各位說再見了。希望各位一路學來收穫頗豐。我們討論過引言、預告簡報內容、目的陳述、架構資訊、運用視覺材料、描述「改變」、回答問題和簡報總結的用語。也學過 prepare 、 practice 與 perform 簡報的技巧。我也介紹了簡報過程中應該謹記在心的實用概念。現在，各位已研讀完本書，如果做過了所有的 Task 、使用過書末的「學習目標記錄表」來選擇 set-phrases 、採用了我提供的 prepare 、 practice 與 perform 技巧，那麼你的英文簡報能力應該大大地提昇了。

記得本書「前言」中有個 Task 要各位從一則簡報片段中找出 chunks 、 set-phrases 和 word partnerships 嗎？現在再作一次這個 Task 是個不錯的主意，可藉此測試你們學到了多少。

Task 1

請看以下的簡報片段及其中譯。然後將 chunks 、 set-phrases 與 word partnerships 畫上不同顏色的底線，最後完成下表。見範例。

OK. This graph displays the sales figures for the last quarter of this year compared with the figures for the last quarter of last year. We can see from the graph that this year's figures are much lower than the previous year's. Let me remind you, however, that these figures are not quite complete. This is because we are still waiting for the results from a sales person who has been on leave. In general, these figures suggest that results this year are going to be comparable to results from last year. Let's turn now to costs, which we can see here.

【中譯】

好。這張圖呈現的是今年與去年最後一季銷售數字的比較。我們從本圖可看到，今年的數字要比去年同季低得多。這是因為我們還在等一位休假中的業務同仁提供某些數據，所以這些數字並不十分完整。然而，這些數字顯示今年的業績和去年相當。現在讓我們來看成本的部分，在這邊。

Set-phrases	Chunks	Word Partnerships
• This graph displays ...	• ... compared with ...	• sales figures

答案 請回到本書「前言」，以「簡報必備語庫　前言3」核對答案，相較於第一次的練習，你進步了多少呢？

各位已經研讀完本書，接下來該作些什麼，才能維持專業的英文簡報水平呢？

許多客戶告訴我，他們不住在說英文的環境裡，或者不是在說英文的環境裡工作，他們很難維持或提昇英文程度。在此我提出一些個人建議，告訴你持續加強英文的好方法。維持英文水平的方法很多，本書可作為各位專注在簡報、口說、和維持一般英文水平的參考書。

操練

1. 練習已學到的知識是很重要的。要勇敢，把所學的新知應用在工作上。許多客戶因為新習得的簡報知識而大獲成功，你們也可以辦到！
2. 在準備簡報以及練習使用 set-phrases 時，可利用附錄裡的語庫以及「簡報準備表」。
3. 每隔幾個禮拜回頭複習各個語庫，確定你沒有忘記如何運用這些用語。
4. 一天至少花十分鐘的時間聽 CD，練習發音。
5. 抄寫 set-phrases 可以讓你熟悉它們，這些時間不會是白費的。
6. 聽取簡報時，不論是英文或中文，不管是以英文為母語者、或非以英文為母語者提供的簡報，都要仔細觀察，想想本書提及的重要概念。你可以從觀察中學到許多。

保持你的英文水平

保持英文能力的方法有很多。我在此提供六點意見。

1. 每天背幾個新字串

你可以從報紙、網上或收到的電子郵件（英文為母語的人士所寫者）中挑出字串。切記在字串上下功夫，也就是 chunks 、 set-phrases 或 word partnerships ，若只是背單字，對學英文毫無意義。

2. 選擇難、陌生或新的字串

記住，天底下沒有難的字串，只有不熟悉的字串。有些字串乍看之下覺得陌生，但是只要多加練習，便會變得熟悉。也有些字串初次看到時不認識，但同樣的，只要多加練習，不久就會吸收成為自己詞彙的一部分。新字串一旦開始運用自如，就表示你已經學會，可以繼續學習下一個新字串了。

3. 刻意運用新字串

利用本書附錄的語庫，嘗試運用其中字串，有益於記憶和吸收，也可以將之轉化成自己詞彙的一部分。

4. 如果可以，盡量避免使用已知和運用自如的字串

大多人總是反覆使用同樣、已知、運用自如的字串，也因為如此，他們的英文永遠停留在原地，不會進步！

5. 試用不同用法，勇於嘗試，從錯誤中學習

用字遣詞會出錯，是因為試圖發揮創意，實驗不同語文的用法，但這是學習語言過程中很重的一環，不容小覷。從來不犯錯，那並不代表你很優秀（除了極少數的例外），實際上只會顯露出你裹足不前，不敢嘗試新語文！

6. 留意生活週遭遇到的語文

嘗試創造一個自己的迷你英文環境。從把最喜歡的網站加到「我的最愛」名單中開始，閱讀感興趣的文章，花些時間將其中的 chunks 和 word partnerships 抄錄下來。研究一再證明，加強英文最重要的方式毫無疑問地就是閱讀、閱讀、閱讀！

感謝你隨我看完本書。希望本書對你有所助益，未來「愈忙愈要學英文」系列將推出更多新書，敬請期待。祝簡報順利！

附 錄

附錄一：簡報必備語庫

你們可以使用本附錄作為準備簡報的參考。在此包括了第一到第九章的語庫。

簡報必備語庫 2.1　開場白與陳述目的　p. 44

開場白 Openings	陳述目的 Statements of Purpose
• Good morning/afternoon/evening, ladies and gentlemen. • Thanks for coming today. • It's a pleasure for me to make this presentation to you today. • I'd like to thank everyone for coming. • Hello, everybody. My name is ... and I represent ...	• I'm going to be showing you n.p. • My presentation today is going to cover n.p. • My presentation today focuses on n.p. • Today, I'm going to be reporting on n.p. • This afternoon I'd like to tell you about n.p. • Today we're going to take a look at n.p. • My presentation today will deal with n.p. • I appreciate everyone's attendance today and hope that you will leave this room with a better understanding of n.p.

簡報必備語庫 3.1 　　標示要點 p. 58

第一點（First）

- I'll begin by Ving. ...
- I'll begin with n.p. ...
- I'm going to start with n.p. ...
- I'm going to start by Ving. ...
- First, I'm going to tell you about n.p. ...
- For a start, I'm going to bring you up to speed on the current situation.
- I'd like to open my presentation today by giving you some background information on n.p. ...

中間的要項（Middle）

- Second, I plan to discuss n.p. ...
- Then, I'll move on to V/n.p. ...
- Next, I'm going to show you n.p. ...
- After that, we'll take a look at n.p. ...
- When I've done that, I'll go on to V/n.p. ...
- Third, I'd like to demonstrate n.p. ...

最後一點（Last）

- I'd then like to conclude with n.p. ...
- Finally, I'll be presenting a summary of n.p. ...
- In summary, I'm going to present n.p. ...
- At the end (of my presentation), I'll be suggesting that + n. clause

簡報必備語庫 4.1　架構 Set-phrases p. 73

- Now, I'd like (you) to V ...
- At this point, I'd like to V ...
- I'd like to turn now to n.p. ...
- I want (you) to V ...
- We need to address two crucial issues: first, ...; and second, ...
- If I could just move on to n.p. ...
- There are three main points here: first, ...; second, ...; and third, ...
- Right now, we're going to look at n.p. ...
- Turning now to n.p. ...
- ... beginning with n.p. ...
- First / second / third ...
- I'm now going to V ...
- I'm going to begin by Ving ...
- Now, I'm going to V ...
- Let's turn now to n.p. ...
- Finally, I'm going to V ...
- I'm going to conclude by Ving ...
- I'm going to finish by Ving ...
- I'd like (you) to V ...
- Let's conclude now by Ving ...
- That's all I want to say about n.p. ...
- I'd like to wrap up by Ving ...

簡報必備語庫 6.1　運用視覺材料四程序的用語 p. 108

介紹投影片的主題 Introduce the Topic

- I'd now like you to look at n.p. ...
- If you look at this (chart/graph/table), you can see n.p. ...
- If you look at this (chart/graph/table), you can see that + n. clause
- If you look here you can see n.p. ...
- If you look here you can see that + n. clause
- On this slide we've got n.p. ...
- These statistics show n.p. ...
- This graph displays n.p. ...
- This next (chart/graph/table) shows us that + n. clause
- This next slide gives us the figures for n.p. ...
- This slide describes n.p. ...

- This slide shows n.p. ...

強調相關資料 Highlight Relevant Information

- As you can see, ...
- I'd like to draw your attention to n.p. ...
- I'd like to draw your attention to the fact that + n. clause
- I'd now like you to look at n.p. ...
- Let me draw your attention to n.p. ...
- Look at the n.p. ...
- Look at the way that + n. clause
- Notice how + n. clause
- Notice the n.p. ...
- Notice that + n. clause
- We can see from this graph that + n. clause

摘要說明關鍵要點 Summarize with the Key Point

- It is clear from this (chart/graph/table/movement) that + n. clause
- It is clear from the general movement that + n. clause
- Let me elaborate on n.p. ...
- Let me expand on n.p. ...
- These figures suggest that + n. clause
- These statistics show that + n. clause
- This slide shows that + n. clause

進行下一張投影片 Move to the Next Slide

- Going on to n.p. ...
- Let's turn now to n.p.(, which we can see here.)
- Moving on to the next slide, ...

簡報必備語庫 7.1　　說明時間的 Chunks　p. 124

現在時間的 Chunks Present (Unfinished) Time Chunks	過去時間的 Chunks Past (Finished) Time Chunks
• this year • during this time • year-to-date • this week • this quarter • so far • until now	• last year • last quarter • during that time • ago • in September • yesterday • then • in 1999

簡報必備語庫 7.2　　說明變化的動詞　p. 128

	完成的時間 Finished Time	未完成的時間 Unfinished Time
向上的動作 **Movement Up**	• increased • rose • went up • shot up • rocketed • surged	• has/have increased • has/have risen • has/have gone up • has/have shot up • has/have rocketed • has/have surged
向下的動作 **Movement Down**	• decreased • fell • went down • dropped	• has/have decreased • has/have fallen • has/have gone down • has/have dropped
輕微的動作 **Very Little Movement**	• remained constant • remained steady • stabilized	• has/have remained constant • has/have remained steady • has/have stabilized

簡報必備語庫 8.1　　總結四步驟的用語　p. 144

Step 1：告知觀眾簡報接近尾聲 Signaling the End

Formal

- I'd like to end by summarizing ...
- I'd like to end by Ving ...
- I'd like to end with n.p. ...
- OK, that ends the main part of my presentation to you today.

Informal

- OK, I think that just about covers it.
- So, let's just summarize the main points.

Step 2：總結要點 Concluding Your Presentation

Formal

- The key issue is whether + n. clause
- In conclusion, I would like to recommend that + n. clause
- There are two recommendations I would like to make at this point. First, ...
- In conclusion, I would like to suggest that + n. clause
- In conclusion, I think we should V ...
- In conclusion, I think we need to V ...
- That concludes my presentation (to you) today.
- I think it's clear that we should V ...

Informal

- So, to wind up, I think we should V ...
- I think I'll stop here.

Step 3：感謝觀眾 Thanking the Audience

Formal

- Thank you for your attention.
- Thank you for listening and for inviting me here today.

Informal

- Thanks, everyone.

- Thanks for listening.

Step 4 ：請觀眾提問 Inviting Questions

Formal

- Now I would like to invite you to ask any questions you may have.

- At this point, I'd be very interested to hear your questions or any comments you may have.

Informal

- So, any questions?

- Right then, are there any questions?

- OK, now you are welcome to ask any questions.

簡報必備語庫 9.1   應答的 Set-phrases p. 161

確定會回答的問題 Questions you know you can answer

- Yes, good point. I think ...

- Thanks for that question. In my opinion ...

- Yes, I understand. As I mentioned earlier, I think ...

- Yes, that's a very good question. It depends on 'wh' ...

- Well, I think I answered that earlier, but to repeat, ...

- I'm glad you asked me. I think ...

- You're right on the money! That's exactly what I thought.

- Thank you for pointing out the mistake here. I'm afraid it's a typo. The correct figure is ...

不確定會回答的問題 Questions you're not sure you can answer

- You've raised a contentious issue there.

- Hmm. Yes. Interesting point. What do you think?

- Yes, I see. What are your views on this before I give my own?

- I'm not sure I follow. Do you mean ...?

- Well, you've raised a very interesting point there. In reply I would like to point out that ...
- To be honest, I think that raises a different issue.
- I think that's a legitimate concern.

確定不會回答的問題 Questions you know you cannot answer

- I'm not sure I can answer that at this time.
- I'm afraid I simply don't know.
- I haven't seen the data on this, so I'm not in a position to give you a clear answer yet.
- Could I deal with that later? Thanks.
- Can I get back to you on that one?
- Perhaps you could write to me with your question.
- I don't know without seeing the figures.
- I'm afraid I can't comment on that.
- I don't know the answer to your question, but I'll make a note here.

附錄二： CD 目錄

CD 軌數	章節軌數	內容
01		版權聲明
02	Track 前言 1	簡報片段
03	Track 前言 2	錯誤句子的範例
04	Track 2.1	6 個開場白片段
05	Track 2.2	開場白 Set-phrases
06	Track 2.3	陳述目的 Set-phrases
07	Track 2.4	連音範例
08	Track 2.5	簡報前言的連音範例
09	Track 3.1	6 個簡報的引言片段（包含預告內容）
10	Track 3.2	標示要點的 Set-phrases
11	Track 3.3	音調的範例
12	Track 4.1	1 個簡報主體片段
13	Track 4.2	架構 Set-phrases
14	Track 4.3	1 個簡報主體片段
15	Track 5.1	高、低資訊密度的片段
16-19	Tracks 6.1 — 6.4	使用視覺材料的片段
20	Track 6.5	使用視覺材料四程序的 Set-phrases
21	Track 7.1	現在時間的 Chunks
22	Track 7.2	過去時間的 Chunks
23	Track 7.3	描述「改變」的動詞
24	Track 7.4	使用「改變」動詞的簡報片段
25	Track 8.1	3 個總結片段
26	Track 8.2	總結的 Set-phrases
27	Track 9.1	7 個問答的範例
28	Track 9.2	應答的 Set-phrases
29	Track 9.3	20 個練習問題

附錄三：錄音稿

本附錄僅包括簡報片段的錄音稿。語庫的發音練習錄音稿，可參見附錄一：簡報必備語庫。

前言

Track 前言 1

OK. This graph displays the sales figures for the last quarter of this year compared with the figures for the last quarter of last year. We can see from the graph that this year's figures are much lower than the previous year's. Let me remind you, however, that these figures are not quite complete. This is because we are still waiting for the results from a sales person who has been on leave. In general, these figures suggest that results this year are going to be comparable to results from last year. Let's turn now to costs, which we can see here.

【中譯】

好。這張圖呈現的是今年與去年最後一季銷售數字的比較。我們從本圖可看到，今年的數字要比去年同季低得多。這是因為我們還在等一位休假中的業務同仁提供某些數據，所以這些數字並不十分完整。然而，這些數字顯示今年的業績和去年相當。現在讓我們來看成本的部分，在這邊。

Unit 2

Track 2.1

簡報片段一

Good morning, ladies and gentleman. Thanks for coming today. My presentation today will deal with the marketing plan for our new product line.

【中譯】

早安，各位小姐、先生。謝謝大家的光臨。我今天的簡報將探討新產品線的行銷計劃。

簡報片段二

I'd like to thank everyone for coming. Today, we're going to take a look at just-in-time management and why we need to improve our efforts in this area in order to stay competitive.

【中譯】

謝謝大家的光臨。今天我們要來看看零庫存管理，以及我們爲何需要加強在這個領域的努力，以保持競爭力。

簡報片段三

Thanks for coming. Today, I'm going to be reporting on the sales results for all four regions in the last three quarters, and setting revised targets for the last quarter.

【中譯】

謝謝各位的光臨。今天，我要報告四個區域在過去三季的銷售結果，並爲下一季設定修正後的目標。

簡報片段四

Hello, everybody. My name is Luca Jarvis and I represent Macrohard. This afternoon I'd like to tell you about our latest product and how I think your company can benefit from it.

【中譯】

哈囉，大家好。我的名字是 Luca Jarvis ，代表 Macrohard 公司。今天下午，我要爲各位介紹我們的最新產品，以及這產品對貴公司有什麼好處。

簡報片段五

It's a pleasure for me to make this presentation to you today. My presentation is going to cover some recent developments in our sister regions, and to discuss some ways to bring our region up to the same level of competitiveness.

【中譯】

今天我很高興來對大家做這個簡報。我的簡報將介紹姊妹地區一些最新的發展，並討論一些將我們地區的競爭力提升到同樣水平的方法。

簡報片段六

I'd like to thank everyone for coming. I'm going to be showing you the latest work from the R&D department, and getting your ideas for marketing these exciting new products.

【中譯】

謝謝各位的蒞臨。我將向各位展示研發部門最新的工作成果，並尋求各位對行銷這個有趣的新產品的點子。

Track 2.5

I appreciate everyone's attendance today and hope that you will leave this room with a better understanding of our market share.

【中譯】

感謝各位今天的出席，希望你們離開這裡時，對我們的市場佔有率有更深的了解。

Unit 3

Track 3.1

簡報片段一

Good evening, ladies and gentlemen. I'd like to thank you all for coming. / My presentation today focuses on why improving your English is beneficial to you. / I'd like to begin my presentation today by giving you some background information on English language education in Taiwan. / Second, I plan to discuss the advantages competent English speakers enjoy in the local job market. / When I've done that, I'll go on to introduce the range of products available to English learners from Lexikon International. / I'd then like to conclude with a summary of my main points and to recommend the best possible solution available to English learners here in Taipei.

【中譯】

晚安，各位小姐、先生。謝謝各位的蒞臨。／我今天簡報的重點在於為什麼改善英文對你們有益。／簡報一開始我會先向各位介紹一些台灣英文教育的背景資訊。／第二，我打算談談說一口流利英文的人在本地就業市場的優勢。／談完這點，我將繼續介紹 Lexikon International 為英文學習者提供的各種產品。／然後我會摘要說明要

點，並為身在台北的英文學習者推薦最好的解決方案。

簡報片段二

Thanks for coming today. / Today, I'm going to be reporting on last year's results. / First, I'm going to show you the results for all regions quarter by quarter. / Second, I'm going to show you the targets set by the regional office for the year in question, comparing them with the results to give you an idea of our performance. / After that, we'll take a look at some of the top performers in each region. / When I've done that, I'll go on to compare our performance last year with our main competitors' performance over the same period. / I'd then like to conclude with a summary of our market position at the end of last year.

【中譯】

謝謝各位的蒞臨。／今天，我將報告去年的結果。／首先，我會一季一季地向各位報告所有地區的結果。／第二，我將告訴各位地區辦公室所設定的去年目標，將結果與此目標比較，讓各位對我們的績效有所了解。／接著，我們將看看各地區表現最好的人。／這部分結束後，接著我會將我們去年的績效和主要競爭對手同時期的績效作比較。／然後我會摘要說明去年底我們的市場地位來作為總結。

簡報片段三

Hello everybody, my name is Larry Chen and I represent Better Business Consultancy Incorporated. / My presentation today will deal with the problems you are having maintaining your market share. / For a start, I'm going to bring you up to speed on the current situation. / Then, I plan to discuss the main threats to your market share and to identify those key factors which you can do something about. / Third, I'd like to demonstrate how your sister region, Hong Kong, has managed to deal with this issue and to see if there are any lessons we can learn from them. / At the end, I'll be suggesting a five-point strategy for dealing with this issue.

【中譯】

哈囉大家好，我的名字是 Larry Chen ，代表 Better Business 顧問公司。／我今天的簡報將探討各位在維持市場佔有率時面臨的問題。／首先，我將帶領各位很快地看過目前的情況。／第二，我要討論各位的市場佔有率所面臨的主要威脅，並找出我們可以應對的關鍵要素。／第三，我要示範你們的姊妹區域，香港，如何處理這個議題，看看有沒有可以向它學習的部分。／最後，我將建議處理這個議題的五點策略。

Track 3.3

簡報片段一

I'd like to open my presentation today by giving you some background information on English language education in Taiwan.

【中譯】

今天簡報一開始我要告訴各位一些台灣英文教育的背景資訊。

簡報片段二

When I've done that, I'll go on to compare our performance last year with our main competitors' performance over the same period.

【中譯】

這部分結束後,接著我會將我們去年的績效和主要競爭對手同時期的績效作比較。

簡報片段三

At the end, I'll be suggesting a five-point strategy for dealing with this issue.

【中譯】

最後,我將建議處理這議題的五點策略。

簡報片段四

When I've done that, I'll go on to introduce the range of products available to English learners from Lexikon International.

【中譯】

談完這點,我將繼續介紹 Lexikon International 為英文學習者提供的各種產品。

Unit 4

Track 4.1

Now I'd like to talk briefly about Asia and three countries in particular, / beginning with Thailand, which for many years had a strong construction industry. For years the Thailand economy was largely dependent on massive construction projects. Although this industry is still very important, there is now a significant emphasis on tourism and, to a certain extent, trade of locally produced goods. / Let's turn now to Korea, which is quite different from Thailand in that it doesn't have such a strong tourism industry for the simple reason that Korea does not feature strongly as a Western tourist destination. However, Korea has a strong manufacturing base, particularly in heavy industrial goods and consumer electronics. That's all I want to say about Korea. / I'm now going to talk about Malaysia. For many reasons, Malaysia is less typical of the other countries in my survey, in that its economic base is far more of an even mix of primary, secondary and tertiary industries. The economy here is more stable, with an equal emphasis on manufacturing, service and tourism. / Finally, I'm going to conclude our look at these Asian economies by summarizing the opportunities they present to the company.

【中譯】

　　現在，我要簡短地談談亞洲地區，特別是其中的三個國家。／從泰國開始，這個國家多年來一直擁有很強的營建業。多年來經濟大多是仰賴大量的營建工程。雖然這個產業依然非常重要，但現在該國非常重視觀光業、對當地生產商品的貿易也有相當程度的重視。／我們現在來談談韓國，這個國家和泰國相當不一樣，韓國沒有強大的觀光業，理由很簡單，韓國不若西方的觀光景點來得重要。然而，韓國擁有強大的製造業基礎，特別是重工業和消費性電子產品。我對韓國的介紹到此為止。／我現在要討論的是馬來西亞。基於許多理由，馬來西亞不若我調查中的其他國家那樣有特色，它的經濟是基礎、次級和第三級產業以相等比例的組合。這兒的經濟比較穩定，對於製造業、服務業和觀光業同等重視。／最後，我將摘要說明這些亞洲國家為公司帶來的機會，作為對這些亞洲經濟體探討的總結。

Track 4.3

　　I'm now going to look in a bit more detail at the results of the survey for each segment of the market. / I'm going to begin by looking at the youth segment. / There are three main points here: / first, most respondents said the product line was relevant to their lifestyle, second, / a significant number said they wanted to own the complete line; and third, / a smaller number said they only wanted one product from the line and had no intention of buying more. / Turning now to the main-wage-earner segment, a much smaller number of respondents said they were interested in the product line, and most of these were female. Most of the people in this segment did not express much interest in the product. / Let's turn now to the senior citizen segment. We had a fantastic response here, especially among women. All the respondents said they would like to own more of the product line, but were not happy with the packaging, saying it was hard to open. / I'd like to wrap up by summarizing the key recommendations from the market survey.

【中譯】

我將更仔細地探討每個市場區塊的調查結果。／一開始我將從年輕族群談起。／在此有三個要點：／首先，多數受訪者表示這個產品線符合他們的生活風格；第二，／相當多人表示他們想要擁有完整的系列產品；以及第三，／較少數的人表示他們只想要這個產品線裡的一種產品，沒有意願買其他的。／現在來看看主要的受薪族群，更少數的受訪者表示他們對這產品線有興趣，這些人大多是女性。這個族群的大多數人對這產品並未表現出太高的興趣。／現在讓我們看看銀髮族的族群。在此族群我們有相當熱烈的回應，特別是女性。所有的受訪者都表示想擁有更多這產品線的產品，但他們對包裝並不滿意，因為很難拆開。／我想摘要說明針對這項市場調查所得來的重要建議，以作為簡報的總結。

Unit 5

Track 5.1

簡報片段一：高資訊密度

Q_1 sales this year were up by 7% as compared to the first quarter of last year. However, these figures need to be offset by high advertising and marketing costs, NT$ 23 million and NT$ 2.5 million respectively. This is a current industry trend and one which is also affecting our competitors, so it shouldn't really have that much of an impact on our overall market share. In Q_2 sales dipped slightly from 7% to 6.5%. The reason appears to be that one of the salesmen was actually taking bribes and selling the product through an illegal distributor onto the black market. This figure shows the adjusted results. In Q_3 we're back up to 7% and rising, and in Q_4 so far we've seen single digit growth in all areas, especially the metropolitan areas in the north and south of the island. However, we are beginning to make inroads too into the rural areas, where demand for the product is slowly beginning to increase, 2% per year to date.

【中譯】

第一季銷售業績比去年同季上升了 7%，然而這些數字仍須扣除高額的廣告與行銷費用，分別為 2,300 萬和 250 萬台幣。這是當前的產業趨勢，而這趨勢也正影響著

我們的競爭對手，所以對於我們整體市場佔有率的影響應該不會很大。在第二季，銷售量從 7% 略微下降到 6.5%。似乎是因為業務人員收取賄款，透過非法經銷商將商品賣到黑市。這個數字顯示修正後的結果。在第三季，銷量又回到 7%，並持續上升。第四季到目前為止，我們看到所有的地區都有個位數的成長，特別是在島上北部和南部的都會地區。然而，我們也開始進攻鄉村地區，這些地區對產品的需求開始緩步上升，至今每年成長 2%。

簡報片段二：低資訊密度

Sales were down in Q_1 from the year before by NT$ 10 million. This is because we did not have a very successful marketing campaign. In Q_2 they went up slightly because we employed an extra salesmen. In Q_3 they fell and so far in Q_4 they are still falling.

【中譯】

第一季銷售業績比去年同期下降 1,000 萬。這是因為我們的行銷活動並不是非常成功。第二季的銷售業績小幅上升，因為我們增雇了一位業務人員。第三季，業績下降，第四季至今業績依然在下降。

Unit 6

Track 6.1

OK. This graph displays the sales figures for the last quarter of this year compared with the figures for the last quarter of last year. We can see from the graph that this year's figures are much lower than the previous year's. Let me remind you, however, that these figures are not quite complete. This is because we are still waiting for the results from a sales person who has been on leave. In general, these figures suggest that results this year are going to be comparable to results from last year. Let's turn now to costs, which we can see here.

【中譯】

好吧，此圖呈現今年最後一季和去年最後一季銷售數據的比較。從圖我們可看出今年的數據低了許多。這是因為我們還在等一位休假中的業務人員提供數據，所以這些數字並不完整。然而，這些數字顯示今年的業績和去年相當。現在讓我們討論成本的部分，在這兒。

Track 6.2

I'd now like you to look at this pie chart, which shows the market segmentation for skin care products. Notice how the anti-wrinkle segment is still almost entirely comprised of a small but cash rich group of mature professionals, while the whitening segment is made up of a broad spectrum of youth and young adults. It is clear from this that there is a market for our whitening products among mature professionals. Moving onto the next slide, let's look at the customer profile of these two segments in more detail.

【中譯】

我現在要請各位看看這張圓餅圖，這張圖顯示了護膚產品的市場區隔。請注意除皺區塊的族群小，但主要都是資金充裕、成熟的專業人士；美白區塊的族群主要散佈在青少年和年輕的成年人之間。從這兒可以明顯地看出，美白產品在成熟的專業人士族群中還有市場空間。進入下一張幻燈片，讓我們更深入探討這兩個區塊的消費者資料。

Track 6.3

On this slide we've got sales results for the last three years contrasted with targets for the same period. As you can see, results have been consistently down from targets across the period. Let me elaborate on this. While you could argue that our sales teams are not meeting their targets, it is possible to suggest that targets — which are set by head office in the US — are unrealistic and do not reflect real local market conditions. Let's turn to a comparison of sales and targets in other regions to see how we compare.

【中譯】

在這張投影片上，可以看到過去三年的銷售業績和同時期目標的比較。誠如各位所見，這段期間的業績一直都低於目標。讓我對此進一步說明。各位可能認為我們的銷售業績並未達到目標，但也可能是目標──由美國總公司設定的──並不實際，而且不能反映當地市場的真正狀況。讓我們看看其他地區銷售業績和目標的比較，以便看出我們的表現如何。

Track 6.4

This next slide gives us the figures for costs and margins for our three main lines in all three markets. I'd like to draw your attention to the fact that there has been a consistent decline in the Easyloop brand in all three markets, while the other two key brands have grown. It is clear from the general movement that the strategy the agency is using for this particular brand is not working for us. Going on to the next slide, we can analyze these figures in slightly more detail.

【中譯】

　　下一張投影片提供我們三大市場中三個主要產品線的成本和獲利數字。我要請各位注意，Easyloop 品牌在三個市場的銷量都下滑，另外兩個主要品牌則是成長。從這個大概的走勢可以清楚地知道，代理商對這個品牌採用的策略並不適合我們。接著看下一張投影片，我們略微分析一下這些數字。

Unit 7

Track 7.1

　　This slide shows the current direction of the market. I'd like to draw your attention to the fact that imports from Japan have increased, while domestically produced goods have remained steady all through the period. Let me expand on this. It seems that consumers have been switching to Japanese goods because of their perceived better quality. Certainly, Japanese branding is more successful than ours. Let's turn now to a closer look at the market segments for imported Japanese goods to see what we can learn from them.

【中譯】

　　這張投影片顯示了目前市場的走向。我要請各位注意，來自日本的進口增加，而國內生產的商品在這段期間則是依然持平。讓我進一步說明，消費者似乎改買日本商品，因為他們認為商品的品質較佳。當然，日本的品牌比我們的成功。現在讓我們更仔細地看看日本進口商品的市場區塊，看看我們有什麼可以效法的。

Track 7.2

　　This graph displays the results for the period under review. As you can see, results did not match the targets, and were unevenly distributed across the four regions. Notice how the Northern Sales Area — specifically Taipei — achieved better results than other areas, with Kaohsiung coming second. These figures suggest that our goods were more attractive to consumers in urban areas. Let's turn now to the previous year, which you can see here.

【中譯】

這張圖顯示了調查期間的業績。誠如各位所見，業績並未達到目標，而且這四大區域的分布也很不平均。請注意北部的銷售區域——特別是台北——如何達成高於其他區域的業績，高雄排名第二。這些數字顯示我們的商品對於都會區的顧客有比較高的吸引力。現在讓我們看看前一年的業績，各位可從此看到。

Track 7.4

If you look at this chart you can see the sales results for our three main regions for the first three quarters of the year, and the results so far for this quarter. Let me draw your attention to the East Region, where sales rose dramatically in the second quarter, and then went up again slightly in Q_3. Sales have gone up again this quarter. This is because we hired another sales person. However, look at the way that in the other two regions, sales went down from Q_2 to Q_3 and have fallen again in Q_4. It is clear from the general movement that we should employ extra sales people in the other regions. Moving on to the next slide, which shows the relationship between ...

【中譯】

如果各位看看這張圖，可以看到我們三個主要區域今年前三季的銷售結果，以及本季至今的銷售成果。請各位注意東部地區，這地區的銷售成果在第二季大幅上揚，接著在第三季又微幅攀升。銷量在這一季也再度增加。這是因為我們雇用了一位業務人員。然而，看看另外兩個區域的情況，從第二季到第三季的銷售成果下降了，第四季也再度減少。從這大概的走勢可以清楚地看出，我們應該在其他區域增聘業務人員。接著看下一張投影片，這張投影片顯示……之間的關係。

Unit 8

Track 8.1

簡報片段一

I'd like to end by summarizing the main point of my presentation. / The key issue is whether we should adjust our pricing strategy to try to boost sales. I have outlined the arguments against doing so, as well as why I think we should. We have seen the result of pricing readjustment in our competitors' sales, and while I am not suggesting that we enter into a price war, in conclusion I would like to suggest that we take advantage of the slight reduc-

tion in production costs to lower our prices. Thank you for your attention. At this point, I'd be very interested to hear your questions or any comments you may have.

【中譯】

我要摘要說明簡報的要點來做為結束。／關鍵議題在於我們是否應該調整定價策略，藉此提振銷售成果。我已列舉反對這麼做的論點，以及我覺得為什麼應該這麼做的論點。我們已看到競爭對手調整定價後的銷售成果，我並不建議我們打價格戰，但總結來說，我想我們應該利用生產成本略為下降的優勢，調降售價。謝謝各位的聽講。現在，我想聽聽各位的問題或任何的評論。

簡報片段二

OK, that ends the main part of my presentation to you today. I think it's clear that we should change the campaign strategy to appeal to the middle segment of the market where we can expect more growth. Based on the market research I have shown you, I am confident that adjusting our strategy in this way will give us the sales figures we need to meet our targets and be the best in the region. Thanks everyone. OK, now you are welcome to ask any questions.

【中譯】

好吧，我今天對各位簡報的主要部分就到此為止。我想我們顯然應該改變推廣策略，吸引市場的中層區塊，我們在這部分可預期更多的成長。基於我剛才向各位展示的市場研究，我有信心以這方式調整策略能讓我們達到目標銷量、也可使我們成為該區表現最佳者。謝謝各位。好了，現在歡迎各位提出問題。

簡報片段三

OK, I think that just about covers it. So, to round up, I think we should go for the blue packaging because our focus groups all said it looks cute. Any questions?

【中譯】

好吧，我想到此差不多報告完畢。所以，作個總結，我想我們應該選擇藍色的包裝，因為我們的焦點團體都說這看起來比較可愛。有任何問題嗎？

Unit 9

Track 9.1

Question 1

Q: Can you say something about strengthening our products in this market?

A: Good question. What are your views on this before I give my own?

【中譯】

問：你能談談強化我們的產品以爭取市場嗎？

答：好問題，在我說明自己的看法之前，你對此有何看法嗎？

Question 2

Q: Can you repeat what you said earlier about the new product range being prepared for next year? I'd like to know more about that.

A: I'm glad you asked me. I think the new range, which will be ready in Q_3, represents a new move forward ...

【中譯】

問：你能否重覆一遍先前提到預備明年推出的新產品部分？我想要多了解一些？

答：我很高興你問我這個問題。我想新的產品線將會在第三季完成，這代表了朝……邁進的新發展。

Question 3

Q: I was interested in what you said about competition from China. What about competition from Japan?

A: To be honest, I think that is a different issue which I'm not prepared to go into here.

【中譯】

問：我對於你談論來自中國的競爭很有興趣。可否談談來自日本的競爭？

答：老實說，我覺得這是另外一個議題，我現在不打算討論這個部分。

Question 4

Q: Why are there no figures for Q_1 next year? The projections are a bit shortsighted, don't you think?

A: I'd like to emphasize here that we should focus on our short-term objectives at this time, and leave the long-term objectives to the regional office.

【中譯】

問：為什麼沒有明年第一季的數字？這些預期有些短視，你不覺得嗎？

答：我在此想要強調，我們此時應該將重心放在短期目標上，將長期目標留給區域辦公室費心。

Question 5

Q: In what are you saying through the target figures?

A: I'm not sure I follow. Do you mean you would like to see the target figures again? Here they are.

【中譯】

問：你透過這些目標數字說些什麼？

答：我不清楚你說的意思。你是說你要再看看這些目標數字嗎？它們在這兒。

Question 6

Q: Why have we not targeted Japan as a market? Surely it's a market we should be trying to enter.

A: Yes, that's a very good question. It depends on what product range you're talking about. For the Sheerlux range, we are targeting Japan ...

【中譯】

問：我們為什麼不將日本市場定為目標市場？它無疑是我們應該試著打入的市場。

答：是的，這是個很好的問題。這要看你說的是哪些產品組合。以 Sheerlux 系列產品來說，我們應該以日本為目標……

Question 7

Q: You haven't said much about the regulatory changes? How are we going to get around those?

A: You've raised a contentious issue there. As a matter of fact, we are setting up a focus group ...

【中譯】

問：你對規定改變的部分談得不多？我們要如何因應呢？

答：你提出了一個很具爭議性的議題。事實上，我們正在成立一個焦點團體……

Track 9.3

1. Could you say a bit more about the main difference between doing a presentation in Chinese, and doing one in English?
2. Why is practice so important when working on a presentation?
3. How can I prevent my audience from becoming bored?
4. What is the key to a successful presentation, in your view?
5. How can I measure the success of my presentation?
6. Can you explain the difference between high and low density information?
7. What's the difference between the audio and the visual channels, and why is this important?
8. What's the difference between signposting set-phrases and organizing set-phrases?
9. Please tell me more about how to design effective visuals?
10. I'm still a bit confused about the Leximodel. Can you explain it again, please?
11. You keep talking about set-phrases. What is a set-phrase?
12. What do I do if the equipment breaks down in the middle of my presentation?
13. What should I wear to make a good impression?
14. Why should the handouts be different from the slides?
15. What's the best way to stand?
16. When I'm doing a presentation, I feel so nervous. Can you help me with this?
17. What should I do with my hands?
18. Do you have any advice for people who have never made a presentation before?
19. How can I improve my pronunciation?
20. Could you explain once again how to use the preparation sheets. I didn't quite get that.

【中譯】

1. 你能不能多談些以中文作簡報和以英文作簡報之間的主要差異？
2. 練習對於簡報的準備為什麼那麼重要？
3. 我要如何避免讓觀眾覺得無趣？
4. 依你的觀點，成功簡報的關鍵是什麼？
5. 我如何衡量我的簡報成功與否？

6. 你能否解釋高、低密度資訊之間的差異？

7. 聽覺和視覺管道之間的差異是什麼？這為什麼重要？

8. 預告簡報內容的 set-phrases 和架構 set-phrases 之間有何差異？

9. 請告訴我更多關於如何設計有效的視覺資料？

10. 我對 Leximodel 還有些疑惑，能否再請你解釋一遍？

11. 你一直在談 set-phrases。 Set-phrase 是什麼？

12. 如果簡報進行到一半，設備故障了，我該怎麼辦？

13. 我應該穿什麼才能留下好的印象？

14. 講義為什麼應該和投影片不同？

15. 最好的站立方式為何？

16. 當我做簡報時，我覺得非常緊張。你能否幫我解決這個問題？

17. 我的手應該做些什麼？

18. 對於從來沒有做過簡報的人，你有沒有任何建議？

19. 我如何改善我的發音？

20. 你能否再解釋一次如何運用「簡報準備表」。我不是很了解。

附錄四：學習目標記錄表

利用這張表來設立你的學習目標和記錄你的學習狀況，以找出改進之道。

第一欄：寫下你接下來一週預定學習或使用的字串。
第二欄：寫下你在當週實際使用該字串的次數。
第三欄：寫下你使用該字串時遇到的困難或該注意的事項。

預計使用的字串	使用次數	附註

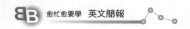
附錄五：簡報準備表

簡報準備表

題　目	
日　期	
觀　眾	
目　的	

你想要使用的 Set-phrases	關鍵內容的 Word Partnerships

隨口溜英文最輕鬆！

★讓你30天跨出會話第一步！

★讓你40天英文從此不結巴！

會話震撼教育－基礎篇

1書2CD 定價：400元 特價：299元

■ 92 則生動對話，模擬真實美語情境

■ 從學校到社會7大會話主題完整呈現

■ 從單字、句型，進階到會話，系統化學習好EASY

■ 搭配純正美語雙CD，讓你聽說皆流利

會話震撼教育－進階篇

1書2CD 定價：400元 特價：299元

■ 800句生活實用句大集合

■ 食衣住行十八般會話能力全操練

■ 自我評量立即檢驗學習成效

■ 搭配純正美語雙CD，讓你聽說皆流利

★讓你45天成為會話高手！

★讓你輕鬆溜英文談時事！

會話震撼教育－挑戰篇

1書2CD 定價：400元 特價：299元

■ 300個道地句型熟透透

■ 5大熱門談話主題熱烈開講

■ 超高頻例句片語一網打盡

■ 搭配純正美語雙CD，培養聽說能力

會話震撼教育－時事篇

1書2CD 定價：380元

■ 16篇國內外重要時事精彩討論

■ 重點字彙快速掌握，重點短句運用自如

■ 模擬對話練習，實際演練學習快

■ ICRT新聞播報員專業錄音，練習聽力更上手

喚醒你的英文語感！

國家圖書館出版品預行編目資料

愈忙愈要學英文簡報 / Quentin Brand作；
胡瑋珊譯. －－初版. －－臺北市：
貝塔語言，2004〔民93〕
　　面；　　　公分

　ISBN 957-729-436-7（平裝附光碟片）

　1. 企管英語－讀本

805.18　　　　　　　　　　　93011226

愈忙愈要學英文簡報
Biz English for Busy People－Presentation

作　　　者／Quentin Brand
總　編　輯／梁欣榮
譯　　　者／胡瑋珊
執行編輯／陳家仁

出　　　版／貝塔語言出版有限公司
地　　　址／台北市100館前路12號11樓
電　　　話／(02)2314-2525
傳　　　真／(02)2312-3535
郵　　　撥／19493777貝塔出版有限公司
客服專線／(02)2314-3535
客服信箱／btservice@betamedia.com.tw

總 經 銷／時報文化出版企業股份有限公司
地　　　址／桃園縣龜山鄉萬壽路二段 351 號
電　　　話／(02) 2306-6842

出版日期／2005年3月初版二刷
定　　　價／350元
ISBN：957-729-436-7

Biz English for Busy People－Presentation
Copyright 2004 by Quentin Brand
Published by Beta Multimedia Publishing

喚醒你的英文語感 ！

對折後釘好，直接寄回即可！

| 廣　告　回　信 |
| 北區郵政管理局登記證 |
| 北 台 字 第 1 4 2 5 6 號 |
| 免　貼　郵　票 |

100 台北市中正區館前路12號11樓

 貝塔語言出版 收
Beta Multimedia Publishing

寄件者住址

貝塔語言出版
Beta Multimedia Publishing

讀者服務專線（02）2314-3535　　讀者服務傳真（02）2312-3535
客戶服務信箱　btservice@betamedia.com.tw

www.betamedia.com.tw

謝謝您購買本書！！

貝塔語言擁有最優良之英文學習書籍，為提供您最佳的英語學習資訊，您可填妥此表後寄回（免貼郵票）將可不定期收到本公司最新發行書訊及活動訊息！

姓名：_____　性別：□男 □女　生日：____年____月____日

電話：(公)_____(宅)_____(手機)_____

電子信箱：_____

學歷：□高中職含以下　□專科　□大學　□研究所含以上

職業：□金融 □服務 □傳播 □製造 □資訊 □軍公教 □出版
　　　　□自由 □教育 □學生 □其他

職級：□企業負責人　□高階主管　□中階主管　□職員　□專業人士

1. 您購買的書籍是？_____

2. 您從何處得知本產品？(可複選)
　　　□書店 □網路 □書展 □校園活動 □廣告信函 □他人推薦 □新聞報導 □其他

3. 您覺得本產品價格：
　　　□偏高 □合理 □偏低

4. 請問目前您每週花了多少時間學英語？
　　　□ 不到十分鐘 □ 十分鐘以上，但不到半小時 □ 半小時以上，但不到一小時
　　　□ 一小時以上，但不到兩小時 □ 兩個小時以上 □ 不一定

5. 通常在選擇語言學習書時，哪些因素是您會考慮的？
　　　□ 封面 □ 內容、實用性 □ 品牌 □ 媒體、朋友推薦 □ 價格□ 其他_____

6. 市面上您最需要的語言書種類為？
　　　□ 聽力 □ 閱讀 □ 文法 □ 口說 □ 寫作 □ 其他_____

7. 通常您會透過何種方式選購語言學習書籍？
　　　□ 書店門市 □ 網路書店 □ 郵購 □ 直接找出版社 □ 學校或公司團購
　　　□ 其他_____

8. 給我們的建議：_____
_____

喚醒你的英文語感！

Get a Feel for English !

喚醒你的英文語感！

Get a Feel for English !